AMARNA EXODUS

I0681042

AMARNA EXODUS

Amarna Exodus

A novel by

Robert J Bridges

Element Press
California

The religions we call false were once true.

—Ralph Waldo Emerson

Chapter 1

THE PROCESSION

SPHINXES crouching like lions and palm trees standing forty feet tall lined each side of the granite road on which the prince and his fellow neophytes marched on their day of initiation. At the end of their procession down the long road dubbed the avenue of sphinxes, they must enter into the pylons of the temple for circumcision and religious training.

The ten-year-old prince unrolled a papyrus scroll as he walked and to his friend Ipy, who would enter the temple with him that day he said,

"We must learn about the gods, Ipy."

"Yes, Amenhotep it will take a long while to learn about them all," said Ipy.

"One is uppermost Ipy, we must learn about the one that created the others," said the prince, handing the papyrus scroll to Ipy.

"Where did you find this Amenhotep?" asked Ipy.

"The people will worship the uppermost one when I become king," said the prince.

"Of all the gods the people admire, how could they worship one over the many?" asked Ipy.

"When I am king, it will be my mission," said the prince.

The prince's naïve mission could be quite a challenge considering the religious customs of Egypt, but he was determined.

Twenty Amen priests adorned tunics and spotted skins of whole leopards around their shoulders, and marched close behind the neophytes. As always, they carried themselves like royalty and their power and influence matched that of the Pharaoh himself. The source of their power derived from a military victory against a foreign invader who staggered out of Egypt in defeat. After the battle was won, the two lands of Egypt— Upper and Lower—reunited and the city of Thebes became its capital. Since Amen was the local god of Thebes, the Pharaoh bestowed gifts of power and influence upon the Amen priests.

The land called Lower Egypt extends from the northern border where the Nile spills from the delta into the Mediterranean and south to the city of Memphis, which is the midpoint of Egypt. From Memphis, the land of Upper Egypt elevates from the cataracts of the Nile south to the borders of Kush. Due to this elevated landscape, the Nile flows north from its source, the mountains beyond Kush, to the Mediterranean Sea.

The Egyptian capital Thebes, located in Upper Egypt, two hundred miles north of Memphis grew rich from the king's gifts of jewels and gold and provisions of land and stockpiles of wheat and barley. In exchange, Amen, through the priests, which were his sole prophets, would cause crops to yield ample harvests and ensure prosperity and stability for the people and protection from foreign invaders.

△△△

Harem girls with braided hair and bangles around their ankles and wrists fanned ostrich feathers around the neophytes to relieve them from the heat. Other girls played with their flutes and sistrums, a musical harmony that pleased the gods. Still others danced between the sphinxes and palm trees, flipping, leaping and laying lotus blossoms on the road along the way.

The celebration in the city of Thebes was for both religious training and their general education and their transition into adulthood. As they walked the mile and a half long road, the prince gazed upon the grand pylons that marked the entry to the temple complex built by his father the Pharaoh Amenhotep III. As he got closer, he could see his father and his father's court along with the Queen Mother and her harem, and all the nobles sitting in the temple courtyard, awaiting their arrival.

The prince was excited that day about the prospects of becoming a priest, which was a requirement for all future Pharaohs. But he was less excited about the other subjects he knew he had to learn—astronomy, geometry and philosophy among them. Still, he was taught that spirituality and learning were connected—that learned souls get liberated from the gravity of the physical world— and in that regard, he recalled the words of a wise old man, a priest from the Ra temple,

The purpose for learning is to liberate the soul for knowledge will set it free

The crown prince came to accept his fate of royalty more and more as he walked toward the holy place. Yet, it all seemed sacrilegious to him, the idea of attending the temple of Amen while remaining devoted to Ra, the god his family worshipped. Amen was a mere Theban god empowered by the endowment of the Pharaohs after the unification when Thebes became a capital city.

Not long ago, as a boy of five-years-old, he was now ten—his mother Queen Tiye had summoned the old priest, Min, to the palace in Thebes.

"How may I be of service to her majesty, Queen Mother of the two lands?" He asked.

"You shall tutor the prince in the nursery of the Great House," said the queen. "You are a priest at the holy place of Ra to whom your queen, the Nubian is devoted. "

"Yes my queen, the god of the sun that rises in the east and warms the land and nurtures the crops and who stirs awake those in slumber, has names and names upon names— Osiris, Horus, Harakti, Aten and Ra," said Min.

Min expressed his joy and gratitude to the queen for the chance to educate the prince, which was an important appointment for the monarchy. For it was the usual practice to reserve the position of royal teacher for a priest of the Amen temple in Upper Egypt. For political reasons they were preferred over the priests of the Ra temple in Lower Egypt for the latter had neither power nor wealth and were unable to interpret the will of Amen. Amen priests were men of wealth and power with much at their disposal. They owned ringlets upon ringlets of pure gold and as interpreters of Amen's will, they commanded at times the allegiance of the Pharaohs.

"The Tools of Thoth you shall teach him now, and later he will gain knowledge of the hymns that pleases the gods, the Negative Confessions, the Seven Liberal Arts and the Ten Virtues," said the queen.

"I shall see to it divine mother, queen of the two lands."

After a day went by Master Min moved into the compound near the palace and since that time, the little Prince Amenhotep waited for him inside the nursery, hour after hour and morning after morning.

Min would test the patience of the prince who as a five-year-old fidgeted about the palace and darted in an out of it in an effort to uncover mischief. When the master failed to present himself day after day and day after more days, it was of no consequence to the prince, free to chase the peacocks or to play with his puppy. But as time progressed without an appearance from Min, the prince began to worry about the absent teacher and wondered if he had missed him while at play. He knew the queen would scold Min for his delay—so after days sitting and waiting, the prince said to his mother,

"Mother, I have waited here for days upon days but the master has disobeyed you, he has not come."

"You're reporting to me something about your own conduct my son," said the queen, "the master will appear when the pupil is ready."

After returning to the nursery the next day, the prince explored the chair that he had sat in for days. It was a replica of a throne made of gilded wood covered in gold leaf, with the faces of lions carved into the end of each armrest. The back panel of the chair depicted Thutmose, his grandfather smiting enemies where the Nile spilled into the Mediterranean.

There was a papyrus scroll on a table at the front of the room, tied with a ribbon, the color of royalty, but he was unable to read the hieroglyphics.

Curious, he wondered about the room to investigate what he thought were oddball things. He studied for a while a scarab beetle contained within a box—a symbol of resurrection, for after the beetle buries itself and lay dormant underground for years upon years, it always returns to life. His attention turned toward a window where two identical flowers sat in identical vases too high for him to reach. He stared at the flowers, unconscious of the passing time, having sat alone in the room for days and days.

A minute an hour meant nothing to him. He was focusing his curiosity at the vases without noticing Min who had entered the room, but he had felt his presence for when the old man spoke the prince was undisturbed.

"Can you tell me young Amenhotep," said Min, in his soothing voice, "which of the two flowers is the real one?"

Amenhotep refused to answer and his focus on the flowers became a gaze of skepticism and then one of scorn, highlighted by the sun beaming through the window onto the African face of the prince.

He was unpleased that after days upon days the master appeared to test him or to dampen his spirits or both. The prince thought it was a question of spite, a deliberate one posed to make him look foolish, as it was his conclusion that the flowers were real— twins perhaps.

The prince wanted to run out of the room after Min asked the question but since he knew the flowers were beyond his touch or sense of smell, he thought to stand on the little throne to reach them. Then a bee, the imperfection of flight, entered the window teetering and tottering about from flower to flower and again from flower to flower. It bumped into the wall, the bee, and hovered near the edge of the window before thumping one of the vases and crashing to the floor and then flight.

Now Amenhotep emulated his father, and stood with the authority of royalty—hands clasped behind his back with one leg forward.

After a good deal of indecision, the bee of imperfect flight landed on a flower.

"There," the shouting prince, pointed at the flower and with scorn in his eyes, looked toward Min"…that is the real flower!"

"Very good," said Min, "Your curiosity and patience has bonded together and become one. It will serve you well as a pupil."
After the master signaled the prince to take his seat, he retrieved the papyrus from the table and handed it over to the boy,

"Amen-Ra is the one god with names upon names. Return now to your father's home," said the master, "You will practice and you will learn the Tools of Thoth, so that you may comprehend this papyrus and other papyri on other subjects."

△△△

When the neophytes reached the granite pylons of the holy place, they entered into a courtyard of attendees, flowers, incense and tables topped with bread and beer of which the neophytes would have none. They stood before the king, queen, harem and court of the monarchy before being ushered to the lake and sanctum of the temple. The ceremony for the audience was near its end, but for the neophytes it was just the beginning of seven years of education.

Everyone was jovial and content that day except for Queen Tiye, who was indifferent about the kingship of her son due to the threat set upon him during her pregnancy. So when Amenhotep was born, it was a relief for her to know that the young prince would become something other than king, as the kingship was the calling of the elder brother Tuthmosis; who was born from a mother of royalty. But when the gods defied her with the death of Tuthmosis, she had no choice but to concern herself with the future coronation of her Prince Amenhotep IV.

After accepting this fate, she fantasized that the prince would grow to be like his father, Amenhotep III, the muscular Pharaoh and mighty hunter, who slain seventy-two lions and forty-six bulls thus far in his reign. Yet deep down she knew her scrawny prince would never hunt lions or bulls, throw boomerangs, or practice target shooting from a chariot. *Her prince was incapable of hunting a lion or bull*, she thought. Yet his power of reflection and fortitude matched that of his father's, and would compensate for his physical awkwardness, she hoped.

In a single file line, they walked through the royal library and down several hallways through another set of side pylons leading outside to the Sacred Lake. One by one in turn, they received the ritual of circumcision, which signified their coming of age. After shaving and ablution in the Sacred Lake, they donned white linens and entered the inner sanctum of the temple.

Chapter **2**

TRAINING

IN THE GARDEN along a path by the sacred lake, the master and prince sat in the shade of a sycamore tree as the sun set in the distant horizon. When the prince fixed his captivated gaze on the setting sun, his mind replayed an inner vision of his first day at the holy place of Amen.

Then the neophytes together sat in a room blindfolded for days, unseeing, unspeaking and unfed. Unknown was the day from night while they waited there to meet their masters. On the third day, sometime after the fourth boy left the holy place in desperation, to satisfy his hunger and thirst, the teachers came one by one into the room to retrieve a pupil and lead him into the garden outside.

Amenhotep and his teacher stopped near the shady sycamore tree and sat there.

"Repeat these words," said the teacher,

"You swear to keep secret all the sacred knowledge," said the teacher.

"I swear to keep secret all the sacred knowledge," said the prince.

"Which you will learn including the seven liberal arts and ten virtues," said the teacher.

"Which I will learn here including the seven liberal arts and ten virtues," said the Prince.

"The soul will then become liberated."

"The soul will then become liberated," said the prince

"Through the pathway shown by the light of knowledge," said the teacher.

"Through the pathway shown by the light of knowledge,"

After devouring water and bread, he waited there in the garden eager to learn but patient, having recalled the lesson that curiosity and patience makes for a good pupil.

The prince deprived of light was eager to see after three days of darkness but after the removal of the blindfold the brightness of the sun made him blink and his hands provided shaded respite. The shadow in front of him became the shape of a featureless man, and then the bronze skin of the man and his features came slow into view. There was a smile with a gap in the center, a sloped forehead with narrow brows—the left one interrupted by a small scar—it was Min.

△△△

The prince was happy that day seven long years ago to reacquaint himself with his teacher. And after seven years had passed under his tutelage, the seventeen-year-old prince had become well learned, having been tested with many old questions and new ones over the course of time, during and in between lessons, some more difficult than others.

"What are the tools of Thoth," said Min

"The sacred writings," said the prince.

"Who was the first man to use these Tools of Thoth?" the master would ask.

"Narmer," said the prince.

"And who was this Narmer?"

"Narmer combined the red and white crowns of the two lands and combined the names of the gods of the two lands—making them one," said the prince.

"What does that signify, young prince?"

"The name of the one god is manifold and innumerable," said the prince, "but just one god watches over the two lands."

"Yes, that is quite true, the name of the one god is manifold and innumerable, but what about the grains of wheat contained within a cylindrical granary with a diameter of nine and height of ten—are those grains also innumerable?" asked Master Min.

"No," said the prince, "so many grains can fit into a granary with such dimensions." The

Prince retrieved a wooden tablet covered in gesso to perform his calculations before handing it over to the master.

"Correct," said the master, gesturing with his hands to form an outline of a triangle,

"Now determine the area of a triangle of land, with a measure of ten on the side and a measure of four in the base of it," said the master.

The Prince erased the tablet and calculated the geometric problem.

"Correct," said the master. He erased the tablet and drew a truncated triangle,

"Now determine the area of a cut-off triangle of land with a measure of twenty on the side of it, a measure of six in the base of it, and measure of four on the cut-off," said the master.

"Correct," said the master after the Prince calculated the problem.

"Now reckon for me, a pyramid that has a base side of 360 and an altitude of 250. What is the cotangent of the area of the slope of the pyramid?" After the calculation Min placed the tablet aside and said,

"Now explain the logic for such a calculation."

"The royal engineers and the royal architects must make certain that all four faces of a pyramid are of equal incline, so they measure the slope in relationship to its horizontal base," said the prince.

Now in the seventh year of lessons under the shade of the sycamore tree, the master said to him,

"Tell me young prince, the names of the seven liberal arts that you have studied long and hard over the last seven years."

"Logic, rhetoric, grammar, arithmetic, geometry, astronomy and music," said the prince.

"Now recite the Ten Virtues," said the master.

After the prince recited the Ten Virtues, the master paced the garden area where yellow lilies swayed in the breeze and a flood of gaudy dragonflies and hummingbirds darted and hovered over the lake.

Min imparted upon the prince great wisdom as a master teacher and was certain to receive praise from the queen for doing so. Although Ra was the one who deserved praise for making him a worthy teacher and bestowing upon him the requisite knowledge and patience,

"Are you yourself proficient in the Tools of Thoth?"

This question was one that Min would repeat throughout the training.

"Yes," said the Prince.

"Now read the papyrus scroll I gave to you twelve years ago, if you have it on your possession," said Min.

The prince was surprised that Min had wondered if one of his favorite scrolls was on his possession as it was something he carried with him always on a string around his neck and the master was quite aware of it. He was happy to gather it, the scroll, which was well worn, and read it aloud.

"Hail to thee, O Amen-Ra...thou hears the prayer of the afflicted, and thou art gracious unto him that cries unto thee; thou delivered the feeble one from the oppressor, and thou judged between the strong and the weak....The Nile rises at thy will...The maker of all that is...The One, the creator of all that shall be. Man and woman has come forth from thy eyes, the gods have come into being at thy word, thou made the herbs for the use of beasts and cattle, and the staff of life for the need of man. Thou gave life to the fish of the stream and to the fowl of the air, and breath unto the germ in the egg; thou gave life unto the grasshopper, and thou made to live the wild fowl and things that creeps and things that fly and everything that belongs thereunto. Thou provided food for the rats in the holes and for the birds that sit among the branches.... Thou One, thou One whose arms are many; all men and all creatures adore thee, and praises come unto thee from the height of heaven, from earth's widest space, and from the deepest depths of the sea....thou One, thou sole One who has no second....whose names are manifold and innumerable." The Master Min nodded his approval.

"Now there will come a day, in the hall of peace, at the proper time, when you must separate your soul from the many sins, which you have committed in your lifetime, "said Master Min, "recite them now from the Papyrus of Ani, as you will then."

"I have not done iniquity to mankind. I have not robbed with violence. I have not stolen. I have done no murder. Not have I made the order for killing for me. I have not acted wicked. I have not defrauded offerings. I have not diminished oblations. I have not plundered the god. I have spoken no lies. I have not snatched away food. I have not caused misery. I have not caused pain. I have not committed fornication. I have not caused the shedding of tears. I have not dealt in deceit. I have not transgressed. I have not acted with guile. I have not lay waste the plowed land. I have not been an eavesdropper. I have not set my mouth in motion against any man. I have not been angry or wrathful except for a just cause. I have not defiled the wife of any man. I have not polluted myself. I have not caused terror. I

have not burned with rage. I have not stopped
any ears against the words of right and truth. I
have not worked grief. I have not acted with
insolence. I have not stirred up strife. I have
not judged in haste. I have not multiplied my
words upon words. I have not done harm. I
have not done ill."

Pleased, Master Min then placed his hands
upon the shoulders of the prince and stared
long into his eyes, searching his soul.

"Your body, a prison house for the soul, is
now a granite temple. Inside the granite
temple, the soul will find a pathway to liberty,
illuminated by knowledge and free of sin."

ΔΔΔ

Min had been more than a teacher he was a
father figure in the absence of the king and
watched over the prince during the nights as
he slept and during the day. He advised and
counseled him in the protocol of royalty and
guided him on the path to righteousness.

The minutes, hours and days of the past six
months of the past seven years under the
guardianship and training of Min had come to
an end, but there was a bit of sage advice to
offer yet, something Min had known but kept
quiet about over the past years. It was the
reason for his watchfulness and brooding over
the prince,

"Beware of those who may plot against you," he informed the prince. "Speak to your mother she knows all about it."

Chapter **3**

A THREAT

THE PRINCE knew all about the threat since his father had informed him about it a time ago. Despite the threat, the prince had become a devout religious man. He endured the rigors of priest training in the seven liberal arts and ten virtues and after acquiring this knowledge his soul may one day seek its freedom from the gravity of the physical world. The kingship and the priesthood were dual destinies for the prince who was hopeful to become a powerful ruler and hopeful to please the gods as a priest in the priesthood.

Despite his requisite training at the Amen holy place and despite what the Theban priests had wished or feared when it concerned the gods, his loyalty and devotion was to Ra and never Amen. For his training under Min at the holy place of Ra was a major influence on him in his younger years.

By learning the Tools of Thoth, he opened up his world to more learning. Ways to reckon a pyramid for example, or measure a triangle of land or understand musical harmony and to write and speak hymns to please the gods. Of course, he had never forgotten his favorite hymn about the sole god with manifold and innumerable names.

Throughout his religious training at both temples, he never forgot the Nubian sun god Harakti whom his Nubian mother Tiye and Nubian grandfather Yuya worshiped. He never forgot the arrogance and animosity of the Amen priests who insulted his mother and spoke against his father, and who put upon the baby prince a threat of death.

△△△

Before Amenhotep was born, the Amen priests made a request of the king, his father, to travel to the lands of Nubia and Punt to secure gold for the temple. They promised that such an expedition would please Amen; and the god in turn, would protect the monarchy from foreign invaders and bequeath upon it wealth and prosperity.

Although the Pharaoh and many Pharaohs before him showered the Amen holy place with manifold riches including land and jewels to please Amen, the greed of the priests had become insatiable. Their ability to interpret the will of Amen had made them very powerful in the Eighteenth Dynasty perhaps too powerful for their own good.

As his father did before him, it was now his turn to contend with the greedy priests, and he wondered why they were able to interpret the will of Amen and not him. He desired to see and speak with the god himself, so that he too could interpret his will. Yet, over the course of time, he became unsatisfied in his desire to see the god and suspended many advisers, as their counsel regarding this matter had been futile.

After some more time, he approached Yuya, for the Nubian military man and high priest had always seemed possessive of much assurance and wisdom. And Yuya did provide counsel to the king,

"If you wish to see the god, you must expel from Egypt all polluted ones," he said.

Soon enough the Pharaoh had acted upon his desire and informed the decree onto the people. By his own hands, he wrote it on a papyrus scroll and royal scribes etched it onto steles at the northern and southern borders and onto the walls of the various and numerous holy places and monuments.

As Yuya had advised, the purging had begun, and with such a disturbance, that it had drawn the attention of the citizenry away from their day-to-day activities. During the diversion, the Pharaoh combined the god

Amen with Ra, made them one and began to construct a temple at Karnak, which he would dedicate in honor of the new god.

The reasoning for his motive was clear, the priests of Thebes could interpret Amen's will and he was unable to. By combining Amen with Ra, he would remove their powers of prophesy—for although they knew Amen, Ra was a stranger to them. Then, the Pharaoh sent laborers and persons of impurity including shepherd outcasts to work in the rock quarry on the bank of the Nile beside Thebes. As prophesized by Yuya, he hoped beyond hope that this would cause the god to appear before him, and reveal to him his will.

The Pharaoh after all, was a man of extraordinary wisdom who had done much to gain favor among the gods. Never had he judged in haste nor punished with excess— but in accordance with the law. He arranged treaties of peace with the Hatte and made an ally of Mitanni, even took as one of his wives a foreign princess, enabling Egypt to live in peace without the constant threat of invasion.

He conquered Syria and Palestine, then, colonized them and appointed Egyptian viceroys to oversee their governance. In the land of Nubia, he built a temple for Amen-Ra and Harakti at the city of Soleb and constructed alters, pylons, lakes and gardens in the god's honor. He built the Sacred Lake to float the barge of Amen-Ra during ceremonies and festivals. He assessed a tax on the farmers' stalks of corn and grains of wheat and barley to present to Amen-Ra; and he sacrificed cattle and fowl at the temple alters on the god's behalf. Now he has purged from Egypt all the impure ones.

The Amen priests mocked my father and gave fright to the queen when she was pregnant with the prince in her womb, thought the Pharaoh—*should thieves and liars interpret the goodness of the will Amen-Ra would have done on earth?*

ΔΔΔ

The loudness of the anvils and the chisels breaking granite was the one audible sound at the rock quarry for the loudness of it quieted the human moaning. With each laborious blow of the anvil, beads of perspiration spread upon the laborers skin like water from the Nile diffusing near the delta. Sweat from the men comingled with more sweat until the moisture covered whole bodies but a cooling breeze from off the Nile gave brief respite from the sun's heat.

Men with unfortunate impairments in their physical bodies struggled with the arduous labor. A blind man held out hope that the nervous blows he struck with the anvil over and over would spare his fingers that grasped the stones and a one legged man crawled to gather broken pieces of rock as it was easier than hoping along or bending about with a makeshift crutch. There were all types of hideous issues of the skin as sores covered the whole bodies of some and a few others including priests from the holy places were as white as snow—lacking pigment whatsoever. The nomadic shepherds were the most unrefined of the whole lot, thieves in desperate need of the palace law, who fed their sheep time after time in the farmers' crop fields.

These were the hundreds of outcasts sent to work at the quarry to please the gods; and the heavy cut rock produced from their labor became monuments and holy places to please the gods also. When the Amen priests took issue with the actions of Pharaoh, sending other Amen priests to toil in the quarry with the outcasts, they decided to pay the Pharaoh a visit at the palace without prior invitation, which was against royal protocol.

Once again, the priests who were full of willful arrogance believed the will of Amen trumped the protocol of royalty. The Pharaoh had heard about the primacy of Amen's will many times before but this time he knew their efforts would fail for after the purging they were sure to loose their lofty powers of prophesy. After waiting in line to have audience with the Pharaoh, he heard the priests.

"You are uninvited and unwelcomed," said the Pharaoh.

"We have come by the will of Amen, "said the priest who spoke on behalf of the rest.
Although the Pharaoh renamed the god Amen-Ra, the Amen priests continued to refer to him as Amen.

"Ah yes, the will of Amen, and what does your Amen long for? "

"There are some who should not be among the outcasts according to Amen's will," said the priest.

"Who might they be?"

"Priests from our holy place are toiling among the outcasts," great Pharaoh, because of the unfortunate condition of a skin that lacks color, as if they were contagious with distemper."

"You use your words upon words as you speak before the son of Amen-Ra, concerning the will of Amen, but who should know better about this desire of him—appointed priest or the son begotten from his loins?"

"Ever since the time the great Pharaoh Ahmose established Thebes as the capital of the two lands, dear Pharaoh, we the priests of Thebes have been the interpreters of Amen," said the priest.

"And the ringlets of gold that adorn the priests' house next to the holy place, and the baskets of wheat and barley alms meant for the temple that you yourself partake of— proven by the layers of fat upon your midway, causing the button of your abdomen to recess deeply—how do you interpret this—your gluttony and fatness?"

"That is beside the point great Pharaoh," said the priest.

"Is your desire to gain riches by the use of the name of Amen-Ra the point?" asked the Pharaoh, "it was Amen's will you said some time ago, that I the Pharaoh shall go to Nubia to retrieve more gold for the temple."

"The mysterious desire of the gods is misunderstood by the Pharaoh who is a mighty ruler," said the priest, "but without the gift of prophesy."

The Pharaoh motioned to a royal taster who presented to the king a golden chalice.

"Remember that the mighty Pharaoh and son of Amen-Ra is also a priest. You have misinterpreted the lord's request to purge from Egypt all of the polluted ones including any among the priests of Thebes, and perhaps including you yourself. You have proven that your claim to prophesy has no standing as you have spoken against the god's will. This court and the future prophesies of you have reached an end," said the Pharaoh dismissing them with a gesture.

The Pharaoh knew the power and influence of the Amen priests had gotten out of hand, as his father, Thutmose had warned him about their ambition and there advantage had always been Amen.

It was because of their ambition and because of the influence of his wife and her father Yuya that he favored Ra over Amen. He sought to appease the worshippers of both gods with the name change but by merging them into one and consolidating their power the influence of the Amen priests increased; and this situation was the opposite of his intentions.

He would have to take stronger measures and as it became clear that his son prince Amenhotep IV would succeed him on the throne, he communicated to him the story of the threat.

△△△

As a young Pharaoh, Amenhotep III enjoyed the pleasure of many wives, but none as beautiful as Tiye, who was the mother of the prince. She was the daughter of Yuya the Nubian military man and advisor to Pharaoh.

One day, Tiye accompanied her father and the Pharaoh on a diplomatic trip to the Nubian city of Soleb to dedicate a temple in honor of Harakti, the Nubian sun god. Smitten was the Pharaoh by her beauty and by her gait, as her bosom swayed like wind in the palm trees. Her respectful, unassuming manner honored the presence of her father that she doted on— attending to his every need.

She was unaware of her beauty and of her sensuality that allured men and that made her more desirable to the Pharaoh. She spoke no words besides the initial greeting and never interfered with the business of the men except for the nuisance of her beauty and her attentive eyes and ears.

After he beheld this gift of the gods for some moments, the Pharaoh knew right away and informed Yuya that he would take her for his wife and she would become his queen, the great royal wife, chief among wives and mother of the two lands. Of course, he was unaware of the controversy this would cause back in Egypt, among the Amen priests at Thebes.

There were many immigrant Nubians in Egypt at the time, and the priests became leery of some of them as they began to exert unwelcomed influence within the kingdom. Nubians worshipped Harakti the sun god and Ra was the Egyptian equivalent of Harakti and chief rival to Amen.

ΔΔΔ

Back in Egypt, there was sudden gossip throughout the kingdom, initiated by the priests, regarding the upbringing of Queen Tiye and the issue of royal protocol. After all, she was a non-royal, and worse, she was a Ra devotee from Nubia.

The priest feared a scenario of a pregnant Queen Tiye birthing a baby boy. The birth would upset thousands of years of royal protocol and convention since a legitimate king must be born from a mother of royalty. What they feared most was the influence Ra would have on the boy if he were to become king, and due to that influence, the possible diminishment of Amen.

It was always about their god Amen, even when the Amen Priests called for the death of her baby boy in the case that he was born, which they claimed was for the sake of royal protocol, and for the sake of thousands of years of convention. And when Tiye learned of this, she became ill during her pregnancy from worry and suffered a long painful labor.

When the queen at last delivered a baby boy, she hid the news of his birth and the baby himself away from the public inside the palace nursery.

Chapter **4**

PRINCE REGENT

SOON AFTER completing his training under Min, Prince Amenhotep enjoyed the confines of the royal palace more than usual. He seemed to notice the paintings on the floors and ceilings for the first time—there were flowers, date palms, lily pads, geese, crocodiles, white clouds and blue skies everywhere. And for the first time he noticed the scent of incense permeating the palace along with the subtle flower-scented breezes from the outside garden.

Located near the back of the palace was a throne room where the king would give audience to nobles who waited with patience in the vestibule at the end of a long hallway. It was a walk of unease and fret toward the king for those wishing to present to him taxes or gifts or request a remedy of one grievance or other.

Upon entering, the visiting nobles bowed and laid prostrate before the king who sat on a throne beneath a golden canopy. The granite lions with emerald eyes and ferocious fangs sat at the base of the canopy while solid gold cobras wrapped themselves around the top of it. Behind the king's throne to his right was a second throne for the queen or coregent.

The visiting nobles, like prostrate statues remained frozen in the throne room and never dared look up until the king began to speak. The prince enjoyed seeing the nobles and priests bow to his father and even foreign dignitaries showered him with gifts and praise on their visits.

He was getting a feel for what the job of Pharaoh entailed, but at the age of seventeen, there was something else that called for his attention more than the court—the queen's harem. And, when Queen Tiye heard news of the young prince and his friend Ipy keeping company with the harem girls, she summoned the king one evening to her sleeping room.

On the edge of the bed, she waited as the king arrived and sat beside her. As he peered through the transparent drapery hung over the bed's turquoise canopy, he admired the pink granite walls and the pearl white floors decorated with butterflies.

"Your son, the heir to the throne has been frolicking around the palace with a harem girl, Senen, the niece of an Amen priest," said the queen, "and after spending time with her they have become close friends."

"Let them be friends. The prince enjoys the company of Senen after many years with Master Min," said the Pharaoh.

"I suppose he shall marry her?" The queen asked.

"A Pharaoh shall have many wives and command a harem of his own someday," said the Pharaoh, "let them share together their games and companionship."

"If he has time for Senen and time for games he has idle time," said the queen," why don't you train him now for the kingship— you won't be Pharaoh forever." The Pharaoh rose from the bed and parted the curtained canopy and said,

"Upon the chariot at full gallop, he should pierce a copper target from his bow or slay three lions for posterity before becoming Pharaoh," said the king.

"Dear Pharaoh, pay attention to your son. His physical prowess will develop later than your own development as a youth, but his mind will pierce any target and slay any lion."

"Then it is decided my queen, but Senen will remain his companion for as long as he desires her," said the king.

"Need I remind the king that Senen is the niece of an Amen priest and that is her sole purpose?"

Ten of the queen's harem resided in the royal palace at the time and most were relatives of the queen or daughters of nobles or high appointees or priests, but none were at all like Senen, the prince's favorite.

Senen was charismatic and while the other girls behaved and bowed according to custom, her disobedience toward the prince amused him and caused the serious prince to laugh at her joking antics whenever he paid any attention. Although she was a year younger than he was, she referred to him as the young prince. She entertained him with her flute and was a worthy competitor at senet, his favorite board game. He sent for her on occasion to play senet some mornings like the present one, after completing her errands for the queen.

"Good day young prince," said Senen, bowing.

"Senen, bowing to me is unnecessary, we are friends," said the prince, "besides you never bowed to me before."

"Yes, I know young prince, but I was scolded by your mother the queen. Some of the other girls informed her out of jealousy I suppose," said Senen.

"I will see to it that they are sent to the harem palace," he said

"No young prince, it would anger her," said Senen, placing a blue lotus flower from the garden into her braided hair, which parted at each shoulder and hung just above her breasts, "I will wink my eye as I bow—so we know that I'm pretending."

"Agreed," said the prince as he dropped the sticks and moved his game piece.

△△△

In the ensuing days, as the Pharaoh and queen had decided to keep him busy, prince Amenhotep IV became full co-regent and took his seat beside his father the king to hear the nobles. One by one, bowing and prostrate, they entered the throne room and pleaded a case.

"The river has hidden the boundary of my crop field, dear Pharaoh, and my neighbor has planted on my land area," said the farmer.

"A clerk shall survey and reestablish the proper boundary. Divided in equal amounts will be the neighbor's harvest after the assessment of the harvest tax," said the Pharaoh.

"I am very grateful my dear Pharaoh," said the farmer as he bowed and backed his way out of the room. Another farmer entered.

"Dear Pharaoh, the great one," said the farmer, "after the last inundation season just before harvest, a shepherd's herd consumed a tenth of my crop of wheat." The Pharaoh looked at the prince and said,

"Prince regent, relieve the farmer of his troubles and give to him your remedy." Quizzical, the farmer glanced upon the prince unconvinced of his capability to render proper judgment given his inexperience.

The prince, annoyed by the farmer who dared to let escape his desire that his case come under the judgment of the older, wiser and more experienced Pharaoh, stood and clasped his hands behind his back to display his authority. This caused the farmer to bow again while on his knees, in an effort to correct his royal faux pas.

"Dear prince regent, I beg of you in your infinite wisdom to relieve my anguish," said the farmer. The prince then clasped his hands in front of him with the two index fingers together pointing at the farmer.

"You shall slaughter one tenth of the number of the shepherd's sheep, and receive their meat and ten vessels of milk for these were nourished by your land," said the prince.

The farmer and many more nobles that day and on into the future was grateful and surprised by the innate wisdom of the young prince as he was given more authority by the Pharaoh to render judgments. A taste of power the prince enjoyed with immensity but he desired more than the problems upon problems brought forth by the nobles.

He had an urge and desire to understand more about the gods who begot the arrogant nobles and who created the rain and snows that filled the Nile that grew the wheat that nourished the sheep. More than a desire, there was a longing to praise and please the mysterious creator for all the good he had bestowed.

The prince had no administrative powers of governance and because he was unable to issue decrees or make treaties he lobbied the king for more power one day while target shooting. On that day, the prince took up the reigns of the chariot while his father beside him aimed his bow at the targets positioned on the dusty field. Horses rumbled on the earth as thunder and arrows sprung from the bows like lightening.

When the king took the reigns of the chariot, the sun beamed down on the dark slender prince as he took his turn at the targets. Although he lacked the sturdy build of his father, he possessed the deceptive wiry strength of two men and his head was even stronger than his body—the force of will Queen Tiye always admired about her son.

Later that afternoon at the royal palace, the prince and the Pharaoh sat in the garden near the pool shaded by the palms of a date tree. Servants fanned them with the feathers of an ostrich and gave them food and drinks to satisfy their hunger and thirst after the dusty outing,

"Father I wished to be assigned as overseer of the temples."

"How do you propose to do so— with the arrow or the bow?"

"With both together if necessary," said the prince, "I could manage the maintenance of holy places and new building projects."

"There are some neglected holy places under the current overseer," said Pharaoh.

"There are many father, and they are overrun with vines and weeds," said the prince, "I would devote my whole attention to such things as it pleases the gods."

"Having been trained in the seven liberal arts and ten virtues; and having been deemed competent in the art of liberating the soul through the acquisition of sacred knowledge, I shall appoint you to oversee the temples," said the king.

"I shall do so father," said the prince, "I shall care for each holy place in the two lands and it shall please the gods."

After his appointment by the Pharaoh, the Prince regent exploited his new authority as overseer of the temples. He honed the skills he would later make good use of as king—the organizing and coordinating of many building and maintenance projects.

He nurtured his focused stubbornness and disposition that consented to no negotiation when it came to the ambition of the monarchy; and he found his calling and gained insight as to the type of Pharaoh he would become.

△△△

The prince toured the temples throughout the land of Egypt, from the city of Annu in the north to the border of Kush in the south, and everywhere in between. While he was moving from place to place to oversee the holy places, he also sought a place to build his own temple as he was unsatisfied by the limited space at the Theban holy site.

Two-hundred miles north of the Theban holy place, the prince along with his architect, scribes and soldiers, came upon a mountain of splendor, with gentle slopes leading toward the Nile's east bank.

The yellow mountain formed a semicircle facing the river with an olive grove at its base and miles of open space for building projects and the sky was the bluest in all the land. Since it was the perfect place for a sanctuary, the prince informed his architect to begin its construction right away.

Although the prince recalled the scroll given to him from Master Min concerning the one god with innumerable names, he was unpleased that his father combined Ra with the god of the enemy Amen priests; so he exchanged the name of Amen-Ra with the name of an ancient sun god—Aten.

"I am the first prophet of Aten," said the prince, as his royal scribes recorded the words onto papyri scrolls,

"I will diminish the Amen priests in a way my father hoped for, for they are the worshippers of the gold that Pharaoh gives them and their religion is the hoarding of it."

The prince was in the process of divorcing the monarchy from the greedy priests at last and for good measure he would for the first time, rename the god Aten, the singular god, and outlaw the worship of all others. During the remaining years of his tenure, the prince continued closing ancient holy places and removing the name of Amen from some others. Although anger among the frustrated priests, as well as the soldiers, nobles and peasants intensified, they were unable to confront the prince as he was under the protection of his father, the Pharaoh, who had many eyes watching.

Meanwhile the Pharaoh himself had an accident after signing a peace treaty with Mitanni and Hatte to secure Egypt's borders into the future. One day, after a long meeting with the diplomats, he retired to the palace bathing room. The muscular physique once present in his youth had abandoned him, as he was now older and unsure of his steps.

The Pharaoh walked first then stumbled into the bathing room before falling and striking his head upon the marble floor, with such a force and irrevocable conclusion on his life's work, he lay there without a thought.

While a messenger summoned the royal physician to the palace to perform surgery, Queen Tiye and the prince regent waited in an adjoining room.

"Dear queen, I have performed surgery to stabilize the king," said the royal physician, "There was a fracture in the clavicle which has been stabilized. I put back into place, a dislocation of the mandible. I stopped the bleeding of a temporal wound that perforated the bone underneath. Rest is all that can be prescribed for now."

All the surgery had been futile, for after the thirty-eighth year of his reign the great and wise Pharaoh Amenhotep III died. The royal burial took place in the Valley of the Kings and the period of official mourning lasted seventy days. During this time, the prince appeared unshaven and shed tears in public places.

Chapter **5**

CORONATION

AFTER SEVENTY days of mourning, servants bathed the new Pharaoh Amenhotep IV, with lime, shaved all of the hair from his body, and anointed his skin with the fat of a crocodile and scented oils. Soon, he would appear before the public refreshed and renewed for coronation.

Curious crocodiles one by one pierced the glistening surface of the Nile, as a convoy of four boats ushered the Pharaoh to the cities of Annu, Memphis, Thebes and Soleb to make known his ascendance to the throne. The king presented tokens of goodwill along the way by releasing prisoners in each city and providing hearty bread and beer to the public.

The coronation was an important but troubling event for the monarchy as the foreign enemy often sensed weakness during such a transition of rule. Because of this, the king dispatched soldiers to the borders to avert any potential chaos, and to reassure any doubters that the new ruler was stable, secure and able to fend off intruders.

After visiting the four cities, the Pharaoh presided over the main ceremony, as predicated by protocol, inside the Theban holy place. But as nobles and commoners filled the courtyard, a bit of ruckus developed outside the pylons as the new Pharaoh began to speak. Soldiers stood in the way of the Amen priests and denied them entry into their own temple.

"The crook and the flail are in my hands and they shall remain there; my pharaonic robes can never be removed; I wear the royal headdress and the double crown of the two lands as I am the son of Ra," said the Pharaoh as attendants placed and replaced elaborate crowns upon his head one after another.

"Several crowns go upon thy head and order shall be retained and chaos stopped at the borders," proclaimed the Pharaoh, "the hungry will be fed, the thirsty will drink of wine, and the naked will adorn fine linen."

The king arose from his throne and shot arrows from a golden bow to the four cardinal points.

"The name of the god is Aten. This is his holy place and I am his prophet—the Pharaoh-god," said the king.

Once a minor sun god, Aten would soon usurp the power of Ra and Amen combined.

Nobles, commoners and peasants alike ate and drank their fill and were satisfied that under the new Pharaoh, they would continue to enjoy the peace and prosperity that was common during his father's rule.

△△△

After mourning the lost of his father and after the public coronation, the new Pharaoh continued his work as temple overseer, closing many of the sanctuaries and sending home their priests. The expeditions by him and his soldiers were missions similar to a charge into battle as horse drawn chariots churned up dust from temple to temple.

There was a dire urgency to destroy the crooked path built of naïve customs and to replace it with the straight and narrow path of truth and righteousness. He believed it had been his profound duty to do so and to direct the misgivings of the people through his informed insight.

He relished the removal of the priests and images of the gods and the closing of the buildings of the gods, including the ancient gods endeared to the Egyptian public. Although he spared some of the Amen holy places, because his mother Tiye, seeking to appease the Amen priests, requested he do so.

Along with him on his missions was his Uncle Aye, the brother of queen Tiye, and general of the military. Although Aye heard many complaints from nobles and soldiers about the removal of gods from the temples, the king was unaware of them. So one day after closing a holy place dedicated to the ancient goddess Isis, and hearing complaints from his soldiers, Aye approached the king and spoke, as he was growing weary of the new king's apparent lack of diplomacy.

"I must inform you of the anxiety of your loyal subjects my king," said Aye, "as you have closed holy places in which they have worshipped their whole lives."

"The gods and buildings are needless and surplus to the divine temples of Aten," said the king.

"Perhaps the buildings of minor gods," Aye reasoned, "but now we shutter the pylons of the temple of Isis, who is most ancient and most revered."

"Isis is said to be the mother of gods but how could that be if Aten gave birth to himself," said the king.

"Your mother and father agreed about the removal of some Amen buildings as his power had once been localized to Thebes, but has since usurped that of the mighty Ra. Yet I see no good reason to remove the holy places of Osiris, Horus, Sekhet, Anpu or Khepera," said Aye.

"Osiris is Horus—the horizon of Aten; Horus is Ra—the rays of Aten and Ra is Aten by another name, which are many and innumerable," said the king. "Sekhet, the burning heat of the sun, is also Aten. Anpu personifies the dawn, which is the light of Aten; and when Khapera rises in the east, it is Aten," said the Pharaoh, who took issue with the long established convention of assigning attributes of greater gods to lesser ones, ancient or otherwise.

"To assume, Aye, that there are many gods and to ascribe to them qualities that are the sole qualities of Aten would be blasphemous but you are my mother's brother," said the king.

"Yes my king, ," said Aye, confounded.

If I could somehow make the stubborn Pharaoh understand, he thought to himself. But despite his efforts, there was no getting through to the king.

His behavior was troublesome for sure, but as they rode forth over the bridges of the Nile and through the valleys between the red and yellow mountains and through the dusty desert past the corn country and oasis of date palms to tamper with the ancient gods, he knew the Pharaoh had gone too far. Oh, but to the Pharaoh not far enough, he went further and outlawed the worship of all gods except Aten.

Chapter **6**

HAREM CONSPIRACY

SOON AFTER enacting the decree, forbidding the worship of all gods apart from Aten, Amenhotep changed his name to Akhenaten and began building a holy place dedicated to Aten within the confines of the Theban religious complex. He himself would often supervise the outcast workers at the quarry and commissioned more labor to assist in the monumental task of temple building.

When he was satisfied that the extraneous sanctuaries of the land were in order, meaning closed, and the irrelevant gods of the land were in their places, meaning expunged, Akhenaten on occasion found time to enjoy his leisure.

Instead of hunting or target shooting as his father often did at leisure, he and Ipy often visited the harem section of the royal palace, to watch the girls and tease them whenever they danced and sang and played music on sistrums and flutes.

During one visit, he noticed the beauty of Senen had blossomed, and she also captured the attention of his royal scribe Ipy, who was also one of his entrusted friendships for his father admonished him long ago that those who befriend him could also betray him.

Senen, the daughter of a noble and niece of a priest had an uncommon beauty of which it seems she was unaware. The sun blessed the brown skin that stood out against her beige linen tunic that accentuated her curved hips and breasts. Her sensitive eyes, alluring smile and full lips had somehow become pleasing to the eyes of the young king.

One day on occasion of the king's surprise visit, while the harem girls were singing and Senen blew pleasant notes from her flute, she became aware of the king's presence, looking over her left shoulder and meeting his eyes. It was as if she felt the warm sensation of his longing glance fixed upon her.

"She looks like a queen," said Ipy. Ipy's words were unheard by the king as he was so enchanted by the girl. So, Ipy nudged the king and repeated what he had said.

"You read my mind Ipy, I will make her my queen," said Akhenaten.

The next day Akhenaten informed his mother about the harem girl.

"Senen plays a flute that pleases the gods mother, I will make her my wife," he said.

The queen walked outside to the garden, pacing her steps and her thoughts back and forth, concerning what she had noticed about Senen through the years. When Senen grew into something that allured men, the queen knew she had been foolish to have her reside inside the royal palace as her assistant.

She regrets that she enabled the prince to fall in love with Senen by inviting her into the palace for his desire to have her must go unfulfilled. She blamed herself for the situation but also her husband Amenhotep III. For the Pharaoh paid little attention when both Senen and the prince were youths frolicking through the palace.

Now inside the palace, she approached her son from behind as he sat in a chair, and informed him,

"Senen is the niece of a priest my son, an Amen priest—she can never become your wife." Many years ago, Queen Tiye had already arranged a union between her son and his royal half-sister, Nefertiti to legitimize her son's right to the throne.

The forsaken love between the young king and Senen became possible when the nobles petitioned the queen to accept their daughters into the harem, as it was a privilege to become a member. Because of the many requests, the King, Amenhotep III built a harem palace to house one-hundred girls.

Of the hundred, the queen chose ten select girls including Senen, Merymery and Taia, to reside in the royal palace several miles away from the harem palace to assist the queen and serve as her attendants.

It was the chore of Senen to go to market for the queen to gather vegetables, fruit, oils or cosmetics. Merymery combed and braided the queen's hair and made-up her face with cosmetics. Taia burned incense each day and tended to the garden outside, and placed arrangements of flowers inside the palace.

Unknown to the prince at the time, the queen had welcomed Senen, the niece of an Amen priest, into the harem as a token of reconciliation.

△△△

The queen had always sought to appease the Theban priests for that threat long ago continued to affect the queen more than anyone had known, gnawing at her during her days and haunting her in her sleep. The nightmare of priests cutting the royal fetus from her womb and impaling it upon a wooden beam horrified her in her sleep and even in her awakened musings, and recurred more often than kinder dreams.

It was because she dedicated her life to resolving their sordid plot, that she arranged the union with a royal half-sister, and admonished her son to spare some of the Amen buildings and to continue financial support of the Amen priests.

Although Akhenaten had honored his mother's request, she feared he had rekindled their wrath by locking the priests out of their own temple during his coronation. The outlawing of ancient gods and closings of ancient holy places added to her worries.

At first, she believed a few spared images and holy places of Amen and the inclusion of Senen into the queen's harem would hold up as tokens of appeasement, but now she was unsure after some priests wrote the following on a stele of a closed temple:

The ancient temples like air and light belong to no one. The king has no right to shutter them, as there is no right to hoard the wind and the moon.

Although her brother Aye had informed the king of the festering unquiet throughout the land, his sage advice was futile. For after hearing about the threat from his father, the young king spared no kindness to the ancient gods. By expunging the beloved gods, and by sparing a few Amen holy places, he hoped to turn the general populace against the arrogant Amen priests.

The queen and guilt were well acquainted for having birthed into the world an illegitimate heir to the throne. It was her belief that as a common Nubian, she should never have married the Egyptian Pharaoh and if she could go back in time, she would reverse the whole arrangement.

△△△

At present, the harem girl Taia went to market in the place of Senen who went missing that morning, and filled her basket with various fruits and an assortment of cosmetics and fragrant hair oils for the queen.

As she inspected some items at the merchant's table, something flashed for a moment into her peripheral view. When she turned to look, she confirmed what she thought she had seen—a priest cloaked in a leopard skin tunic. It was quite unusual to find a priest at the market, and this one was speaking to a girl, who was unrecognized by Taia from the distance where she stood.

After the girl had listened to the priest with much focus, Taia noticed him placing a satchel around her neck and handing over to her a golden ringlet, about three inches across. She recalled that Nubians often presented this kind of opulent ringlet to royalty on their diplomatic visits.

Later that evening after everyone retired to sleep, one of the girls walked out of the harem room, and meandered through the darkened palace, as if sleepwalking—holding her arms outstretched in front of her, feeling her way against walls and around corners. The occasional flicker of burning lanterns helped her navigate her way.

The shadowy girl hesitated at the doorway of her destination to retrieve yet another lantern on a mantle along the wall. She hesitated at the doorway, after seeing the emerald eyes and ferocious fangs of the red granite lion inside the throne room. The nervous flame-light revealed also the golden cobras, which were poised to strike if she dared enter.

Brazen, she climbed upon the throne and sat for a moment. Then, from a cabinet on the far side of the room she retrieved the deep golden chalice and poured into it something powdery from her satchel. The lantern in her hand caused the shadows to dance upon the walls as she moved about, replaced the chalice and found her way to the exit.

The next day, after the king's audience with the nobles in the throne room, the royal taster went through his normal ceremonial routine. With the clap of his hands, a servant bearing a vessel of water filled the king's golden chalice.

The taster poured water from the golden chalice into a smaller white one and drank from it, in front of the king. The long held custom informed the present nobles, after the king drinks from the golden chalice that court would soon conclude.

It had been an audience of futility with the nobles that day for the king had no intentions toward remedy. They complained about the closed temples and expunged ancient gods on behalf of the unemployed priests and the silent soldiers who stood guard at the pylons of the closed places. Happy to conclude the audience with the nobles, he signaled the taster who placed the chalice on a table beside the king. After a few parting words, the king rose the chalice to his mouth as the royal taster collapsed.

Instead of drinking, he breathed in the aroma from the morbid chalice suspended on his lip and replaced it on the table before summoning the guards.

"Go unspoken and escort the nobles out of the palace," said the king, summon the royal physician at once."

Guards detained the old water bearer, while others attended to the royal taster as frothy foam slithered from his mouth. When the physician arrived, and attempted to count the pulse timed by a water clock, it was too late, the taster was dead.

"He drank from the golden chalice," sad the king, handing it to the physician.

"A subtle, bitter taste of poison," said the royal physician, after tasting and spitting out the water. "Perhaps the wells were poisoned my king."

"Take a polluted individual from among the prisoners and test the well from which the bearer drew water," said the king to the sentry.

By the king's orders, every person and every personage vacated the palace, and after having tested the water from the well, the king discussed the case with Queen Tiye and Ipy, his good friend and royal scribe.

Because of the testing, the king ordered the release of the royal water bearer when the investigation got underway, as he was an elder and had been a loyal servant to the king and his father before him, but Ipy objected,

"He fetched the water from the well," said Ipy.

"The well water was tested and deemed clean and the water bearer is a loyal servant with many years of service and no motivation to poison the Pharaoh," said the king.

"Then it was the taster," said Ipy.

"The royal taster received no benefit by killing himself," said the queen, "the water bearer and the royal taster both had an opportunity but they both lacked any motive."

"Perhaps it was a servant?" Ipy asked.

"The servants sleep outside the palace at night," said the king, "but the harem girls, ten of them, sleep inside the palace."

The queen paced the room and turned with sudden reproach toward her son.

"How could you imply that the queen's harem could be responsible for an attempt on the king's life," asked the queen, "they're girls—the daughters of nobles, that can seldom accomplish their menial chores, no less a plot on the king."

"It must be considered queen mother, as there are no other suspects," said the king, "no person came between the water-barer who poured the water and the taster who tasted it before my eyes."

"Perhaps, my king, someone came between them at night and planted the poison inside the chalice," said Ipy.

"Yes Ipy, under the cover of darkness," said the king.

"The harem sleeping room must be searched from top to bottom and each girl searched and interrogated at once," said the queen.

During the search, a sentry discovered a golden ringlet that was untraceable to any girl as it was under a vacant bed.

The next day, the king along with the queen and Ipy interrogated the ten harem girls one by one, concerning the poisoning of the royal taster. Of the ten, Taia, Senen and Merymery had information useful to the investigation and faced more questions at the scene of the crime, inside the Throne room:

"Taia, what did you see at the market on the day of the murder," asked the king.

"I saw a girl at the market talking with a man, a priest dressed in a leopard tunic. He placed a satchel around her neck and gave to her a fine golden ringlet," said Taia.

The queen always removed her crown when she got angry and forgot about the proper behavior expected of royalty, so she hurled her crown to the floor and clutched her face between her hands. The nightmare she had dreamt for many years had begun in reality.

"Describe this ringlet, Taia," said the king, looking at his mother.

"It was about three or four inches across," said Taia, "a Nubian ringlet of gold."

"How did she dress, can you describe her clothing?" Ipy asked.

"Her hairstyle?" interjected the queen.

"She wore a long tunic—white in color," said Taia looking at her friend Senen's long braids, "and she wore a scarf."

"Is it your normal chore to go to market, Taia?" asked the king.

"No my king, I gather flowers from the garden and bring them into the palace, but I was sent to market that day by the queen," said Taia.

"Senen was summoned to go to market but was unavailable. And your whereabouts that morning Senen?" asked the queen.

"I went to gather fruit in the garden for the queen. Many were unripe but I continued to search high and low," said Senen.

Ipy looked at the king.

"Merymery was there any disturbance, even the slightest, inside the harem sleeping room the night before the murder?" asked Ipy.

"I noticed Senen when she woke in the middle of the night and walked out of the room while everyone was sound asleep," said Merymery. Senen stared long at Merymery beside her.

"I went to the bathing room," said Senen, "and when I returned to my bed, I saw Merymery across the room hiding something under the vacant bed—a golden ringlet, which sparkled in the dim light of night," said Senen.

"She lies," shouted Merymery, "I never possessed a golden ringlet of any kind! I swear this to the lord of the two lands and to the royal scribe and queen mother," said Merymery.

After the interrogation, the king, queen and Ipy talked among themselves regarding their prime suspects.

"What priest would dare corrupt the harem with the king's own gold," asked the queen, holding aloft the golden ringlet.

"Merymery was in possession of it," said the king.

"The king may doubt the guilt of the well proportioned Senen, but Merymery possessed the ringlet only by Senen's words," said Ipy.

The queen changed the subject in a flash, knowing how the king felt about Senen.

"Perhaps it was Taia—perhaps she spoke to the priest at the market," said the queen.

"Leave them in the palace as normal and speak no other word of this," said the king.

The king's passive behavior in this matter was peculiar and the obvious fact that one of the girls was involved in the murderous plot was of no value to him. He focused instead on an old enemy—the Amen priests.

"I shall withhold the financial support of them and close their remaining holy places," said the king, "they tried to murder the son of Aten, the Pharaoh-god, but I shall live forever—in the undying field of peace."

Chapter 7

AMARNA CITY

AFTER A SORDID harem conspiracy, the king resolved to abolish all of the gods and sanctuaries and the priests that were disloyal to Aten. He even removed the god Amen from his father, Amenhotep's funerary cartouche; and already had replaced his own name Amenhotep IV with a new name—Akhenaten.

He dispatched sculptors to chisel away the names and images of the gods from the mountaintop monuments and valley tombs, from every stele, pylon and obelisk within the north to south borders and east to west horizons. Soldiers continued shuttering at a fevered pace, the holy places of their youth, and evicted priests who their own families knew well.

The king confiscated gold and jewels from the holy places and removed stockpiled barley and wheat from the temple granaries and in all of Egypt, the king let stand one Amen temple at Thebes.

Meanwhile, after four years of construction the new Aten temple was completed and stood at the base of the crescent shaped yellow mountain near the Nile. Many other buildings, bridges, obelisks and monuments accompanied the holy place, and would soon comprise a whole city. In fact, it became the king's new capital city, which he called Amarna.

The Aten holy place itself was a grand one, measuring 900 feet by 2700 feet, with several pylons leading to a grand hypostyle hall; the extravagance of the holy place was beyond any other. The temple roof was open in the center and the east side to allow in the sunlight as Aten rises in the horizon. The decorated courtyard with palm trees, flowers and ponds and the porticos decorated with paintings and bas-reliefs led to the pylons of the inner sanctum and alter where religious sacrament took place.

Close to the temple and across a fishing pond from the king's house, was located the royal palace. Near the king's house, wild olive trees intermingled and crossed each other like bushes and weeds. Next to the grove were open fields of virgin soil and granaries to cultivate crops and to store them after harvest.

A processional avenue, bordered by palm trees and occasional offering tables on the east, and the blue waters of the Nile River on the west, led several miles from the southern boundary of the city direct to the temple pylons.

At the eastern boundary of the city, stepped terraces led to a necropolis atop a foothill at the base of the subtle sloping mountain. Over the mountain, eastward across the Red Sea, was the mountain and peninsula of Sinai. Further north the Red Sea transformed into a narrow, shallow inlet at low tide.

This was Amarna, the new capital of the monarchy, where the king and Nefertiti would raise their family and worship Aten in peace away from their adversaries.

Although the king appointed himself the sole prophet of Aten, it was his belief that the god belonged to everyone, regardless of name or tribe. That Aten created the entire world and through his rays of light, sustained life in every land: Egypt, Nubia, Hatti, Mitanni and Palestine. And that he was the god of all things without exclusion friend or enemy, domestic or foreign, herd or flock, as described in the hymn the king composed in praise of the Aten,

How many are your deeds, though hidden from sight, O Sole God beside whom there is none! You made the earth as you wished, you alone, All peoples, herds, and flocks; All on

high that fly on wings, The lands of Khor and Kush, The land of Egypt.

△△△

Although engineers artisans and laborers were still busy constructing Amarna, an emergency caused the royal family to move there before its completion due to a public outcry—a rejection of the king as the legitimate ruler of the land. The old charge by the meddling Amen priests had resurfaced and the past appeasements offered by Queen Tiye were fruitless.

The threat had never dissipated in reality but remained like a song, a soft whistle in the wind, a tune of death heard by the queen during her sleep. Now the subtle noises of the power mongering priests, bellows throughout the land.

It was the reason that the king rejected Amen and the Amen priests, and turned to Aten and built the new capital. Their rejection of him, their threat to murder the son of Aten turned him away and motivated the king to achieve what they had feared—the dominion of a god over their own. The baby grew up to be king and the king made Aten the sole god in all the land and himself the sole prophet. If they had killed the baby as they had planned, Aten would be of no concern yet it was never too late to hatch another plot.

It involved pure ringlets of gold again, but this time for bribing disgruntled soldiers, who were angered at the site of the shuttered temples, and declining compensation for their military service. Because of the king's neglect of his administration duties, extracting fewer taxes from farmers and bartering less gold from Kush, he was unable to compensate the soldiers in a fair way and this intensified their discontent.

If swarming insects by chance devoured the farms, the depleted stockpiles of grain would cause famine and commoners and peasants could die from hunger. The old Pharaoh, the father of the new, understood this well and planned for emergencies while Akhenaten the son paid little attention to matters other than religion.

At present, the citizens were hungry for things other than food also; they were hungry for spiritual satisfaction and the stability that went away with the shuttered sanctuaries and exiled gods. They grew angry, angry enough to join ranks with the defrocked priests and unhappy soldiers against the king and against the entire monarchy.

ΔΔΔ

One day a loyal soldier informed Aye the general of the military and uncle to the king, of a plot to murder the king. Priests, he told, bribed soldiers with gold and a few soldiers offered up their services in exchange for the precious ringlets.

"The threat is imminent. Unnamed soldiers disloyal to their general are seeking the demise of the king," said Aye.

"How many are their numbers?" asked the king.

"There numbers are few, but there is growing disquiet even among my loyal soldiers. The few have joined the many; the disgruntled mass of priests, commoners and peasants," said Aye, "Although it is an alliance which can be defeated, perhaps we should dispel tension in Thebes."

"The military general, I presume, still has command over his soldiers?" the king doubting.

"They remain quite loyal my king, I assure you," said Aye unconvinced, "but perhaps the king and the entire court of the monarchy and its loyal subjects should sojourn to Amarna with immediacy and fortify it." Aye spoke this with calm—a tone that belied the gravity of the situation.

The soldier's turn against the king loomed ominous for the monarchy, for the soldiers were the one buffer of protection between it and the Amen priests.

△△△

Once again, a seeming fate interrupted another plot to murder the king, although the king himself was unconvinced of any real gravity—that there was any real plot at all. After all, the murder of the taster could have been an isolated incident, an incident that some may try to exploit for their own advantage.

He questioned the motive of his own Uncle Aye the military general because he allowed priests to bribe his soldiers against the monarchy. Even though his father often warned him that those closest to him might turn against him, Queen Tiye who would never turn against him was able to persuade her son to heed his uncle's advice.

The relocation of the royal family and their entire court to the new capital proceeded in order and the king sent messengers throughout the land for the sake of dissolving any misconception of weakness. It was necessary to convey to the people that the king had planned for the move years ago when builders laid the first cornerstone of the Aten temple.

The messengers admonished the royal subjects to live in peace and avoid rebellion for the king would run a painful rod of death through the spine of any rebel. He alone on his silver chariot would put down a thousand enemies, for he was the son of Aten—the unmoved one.

The king let it be known that he was also unmoved by revolt or rumors of revolt, as he was the Pharaoh-god, worshipped as the living god on earth. He detested his uncle and general of his military, Aye, for presuming that he was anything less. The notion that he would retreat out of the fear of revolt made him question the general's loyalty and wonder had he been involved in the secret plot, despite the admonishment by the queen on the subject.

The queen-mother Tiye remained at the royal house in Thebes where she continued running interference between the monarchy and the Amen priests, but Queen Nefertiti and her harem and the king and his court sojourned to the new capital Amarna.

The administration of the monarchy consisted of the judicial court, which determined who were rightful heirs of property or estates. Charioteers, bowman and soldiers fell under the auspice of the commander-in-chief or general of the military. Heading religious matters was the high priest of Aten, who in normal cases would also command over high priests of other gods and lesser priesthoods, but those have all but dissolved.

The treasury department oversaw foreign trade in gold, and taxed stockpiled granaries and heads of cattle. An important part of the monarchy was its bureaucratic workers, which enabled departments of the monarchy to run with efficiency.

Royal physicians carried their surgical papyri, instruments and medicines; architects and engineers carried their building plans and mathematical papyri; astronomers, unable to relocate their observatories, carried thousands of years of recorded astronomical data. Masons, farmers, weavers, carpenters, bakers, musicians, sculptors, scribes and artisans of all kinds packed their tools of trade and relocated to Amarna.

Chapter **8**

KING'S HOUSE

THE KING, without conceding to the fact, needed to fortify the new capital city with urgency but wondered if he could trust his own soldiers to carry out the task. After much contemplation, he decided upon a course of action. It was an action his father had taken as king—the conscription of several regiments of Nubian soldiers and fierce bowman into the monarchy. After a thorough vetting, which the king insisted on, Aye would also dispatch to the new capital, many of his own loyal soldiers.

When the Nubian military regiment consisting of the finest bowman in the world along with General Aye's soldiers fortified and secured the new city of Amarna, order again established itself after the long sojourn and settlement.

After the conscription of the Nubian bowmen and the fortification of the new city, the royal family enjoyed their private time at the king's house, away from the stern etiquette of royal protocol in Thebes. Built adjacent to the olive grove, the three-story house, although quite lavish, was much smaller than the royal palace.

There was a view of the Nile from the roof terrace and the olive grove and the queen's pond, which the king built for Nefertiti and stocked with fish. It became a favorite watering hole and sanctuary for fowl of all sorts, including the flashy pink flamingoes and peacocks, which the queen and girls adored.

They enjoyed playing the hiding game, secreting away from each other within the tangle of wild olive trees and displaced mountain boulders. They meandered through the olive grove on occasion to visit the flamingos at the pond. The pink beauties seemed to admire their own reflections in the surface of the lake, but in reality, their focus was on the fish underneath it.

Peacocks enjoyed their strut around the pond or the shade trees in the front of the king's house until a fat cat gave chase along with an old dog who between dashes here and there limped on a lame foot.

In all, the king and queen had enjoyed life in their new home along with their two daughters Meryaten and Meketaten and their nine-year-old son Tutankhaten. Nefertiti and the girls lived on the first floor just above the basement, which had four sleeping rooms, a lavatory, bathing room and a dressing room, where the girls enjoyed braiding each other's hair and applying cosmetics.

The second story of the king's house consisted of a dining room and reception area where the king and queen would entertain visitors for dinner parties, games and music. There was also a bathing room and two large bedrooms for the king and his son Tutankhaten.

On the roof terrace, the king and queen enjoyed working in the garden or setting off casual banter about their family or state of the monarchy. It was their favorite part of the house, because from the terrace they could see the rising sun over the yellow mountain to the east and the river on the west. On the north between the king's house and royal palace were golden fields of barley, on the south, a green olive orchard and the pond of pink flamingoes,

"What should we do about the barley fields?" asked Nefertiti as Ipy wrote on his gesso tablet.

"It should be harvested very soon my queen, before the shepherds destroy it," the king said.

"Those shepherds that trespass our borders are undiplomatic types. How shall they, even as slaves behave themselves in the presence of us? It is no wonder to me why your father sent them to labor in the quarries with the polluted ones," said Nefertiti.

"Yes my queen," said the king, "they are most destructible to the fields—like moths to linen, and warlike even with slings and rocks as weapons."

"And the priests, whom your father, the king, bestowed with treasure, should be obedient and filled with joy. But you can never imply such notions upon them, as they are without any part of decency without the king's law."

"Did they challenge Narmer who combined the two crowns and the two gods of the north and south and made them into one god under a united Egypt?" asked the king.

"Do they speak against Ahmose who defeated and expelled the shepherds, and bequeathed upon the Theban holy place, the spoils of war?" asked Nefertiti.

"Do they condemn my father Amenhotep III when he empowered Amen by conjoining him with Ra and forming one god out of two?" asked the king.

"Yet the sole god Aten, who begot the mighty Pharaoh-god—his one prophet, goes unrecognized by them?" asked Nefertiti.

"They will recognize Aten in due time my queen and I as his prophet. He is the one creator, although the Amen priests or distant foreigners may call him by another name because of his multitude of names. He remains the one and one. The creator of the people in all of the lands of Kemet, Kush, Punt, Canaan and Hatti, and the sea people and the wondering shepherds."

"He created the cattle and fowl of flight and fish to swim. He created the fields of corn, wheat and barley to feed them; and the rains and the river of Kush to quench their thirst. When he rises in the eastern horizon, he wakens all that he created; and when he sets in the western horizon to rest, all that he created also rests. He belongs to no locality, temple, nation, tribe or family. Those are the jurisdiction of lesser ones. He is unlimited by any philosophy or ill-conceived notion of any man. The creator is beyond anything man can conjure up, connive or contrive; he is unseen and speaks to his one prophet. He is the noise and the silence; he is simplicity but yet profound; he is infinite and finite; he is science and art; he is an unmoved mover and merciless to those seeking to limit him to any singular nation, city or tribe who claim him as their own," said the king.

Ipy the royal scribe recorded the king's words for posterity with his handy Tools of Thoth.

Every part of the king's day-to-day life before the relocation, had been set to a stringent routine under the strict protocol of the Theban capital— even the time he spent in bed with the queen.

In Amarna, the majority of the king's time was preoccupied with matters of religion, which left little time for civil administration. At present, he was able to attend to some finer spiritual details in Amarna, such as reading the ancient books or writing hymns to the gods. On one occasion, he read something profound from an ancient papyrus, which had to do with his own image and legacy as the son of Aten.

△△△

Once upon a time, in the Eighteenth Dynasty, a queen named Hatshepsut ruled the land. Although she was a dream to look at, for the sake of posterity she instructed the royal sculptors to fashion into stone the image of her with the crook and flail of a king and a royal beard.

She wore the king's crown and sat upon the king's throne and was a most profound warrior, having defeated and subdued many foreign enemies; and she herself joined with her soldiers in battle, unlike some kings who left the fighting to the soldiers.

She was unconcerned about her beauty and more concerned about her status and legacy as a powerful and formidable king, so she adorned the false beard, which she described as the *beard of Ra under the eyes of Isis*.

Queen Hatshepsut was curious about and most fond of a fellow queen from the land of Punt, located southeast of Kush where the Red Sea comingled with a wider ocean.

Hatshepsut received perfume, incense trees, and many exotic animals on previous occasions from the Queen of Punt and wanted to return the favor with gifts of her own. So she sent her soldiers on an expedition to the perfumed land.

Scribes accompanied the soldiers to record the monumental excursion. Upon their return, Queen Hatshepsut was eager to receive gifts in return and more eager to see the scribes' artistic renderings of the queen, as she had heard much about her but had never laid eyes on her.

But the Queen of Punt disallowed the artful renderings of her likeness unless the scribes recorded for posterity, these, her words,

My eyes are from a great aunt; my arms form my father; my hips and buttocks from my mother; my legs and breasts from my grandmother. The aesthetic taste of the gods is pure and magnificent as they took these body parts from several sources and fashioned with abundance the beautiful Queen of Punt.

Although mounds of flesh hung from the body of the queen, Hatshepsut admired her beauty and confidence. She commissioned her sculptors to etch the likeness and the words of the fat queen upon a new portico constructed to commemorate the expedition.

ΔΔΔ

This story of the fat queen reminded King Akhenaten of a hymn he had read as a young boy under the tutelage of Min. It was a very ancient hymn to Osiris contained within the papyrus of Ani.

As a youngster, upon a visit to the royal library, a clerk record keeper of past events, located for the prince, the passage within the Papyrus of Ani. All young men of the Eighteenth Dynasty were encouraged to read, and for Akhenaten it was a requirement. He enjoyed learning about the old kings and their dynasties and about the ancient gods and their holy places:

My hair is the hair of Nu. My face is the face of Ra. Mine eyes are the eyes of Hathor. Mine ears are the ears of Ap-uat. My nose is the nose of Khent-sheps. My lips are the lips of Anpu. My teeth are the teeth of Khepera. My neck is the neck of Isis, the divine Lady. My hands are the hands of Khnemu, the lord of Tattu. My forearms are the forearms of Neith, the lady of Sais. My backbone is the backbone of Sut. My privy member is the privy member of Osiris. My breast is the breast of the awful terrible one. My belly and backbone are the belly and backbone of Sekhet. My buttocks are the buttocks of Horus. My hips and thighs are the hips and thighs of Nut. My feet are the feet of Ptah. My fingers and leg-bones are the fingers and leg-bones of Uraei. All members of my body are members of some god.

At present, the king had decided, after much thought and consideration of the likenesses of Hatshepsut and the Queen of Punt, that the parts of him shall be depicted as a myriad of gods forming the whole son of Aten, for posterity. Although the unrealistic displays of his likeness bore little resemblance to him, they were of a spiritual significance as they symbolized the fusion of the gods into one. For the royal sculptors, the unique art became the accepted form of displaying the royal family in Amarna.

The question of whether the king through his new religion and new art had swayed too far from convention and whether the entire monarchy could be taken with seriousness was uppermost among the nobles. Even his Queen Nefertiti had reason to wonder on occasion about the legacy of the royal family. After noticing a completed bas-relief inside the Aten temple, she summoned the royal sculptor to the palace.

"The king cannot be displayed with such gross irregularity of form," said the queen, "it is a mockery of the king and the royal family, you must change it at once."

"My queen, please confer with the king, for these human parts of the king are from the gods and will be etched upon the walls and carved into stone," said the sculptor.

"Stop what you are doing at once," said the queen.

Later that afternoon, Nefertiti did indeed confront the king. Before she did, she brooded and she wondered about what possible reason the king would give for allowing his form, as the Pharaoh-god, to undergo such desecration. She thought maybe the king was unfamiliar with the art, and the whole thing was due to the artistic shortcomings of the aged royal sculptor's diminished skills.

Before she questioned the king, she asked him to walk with her to the Aten temple.

Along the way, she passed a flower garden and stopped by a walled fountain surrounded by handsome bas-reliefs of Queen Tiye and Amenhotep III. Then walking inside the holy place, she stopped with abruptness before the bas-relief in question and waited for an explanation. When she noticed there was none forthcoming, she spoke to the king.

"Are you pleased with this?" asked the queen.

The parts of the king that comprised his whole body were disproportionate from his actual physique. The long slender neck sat atop a skinny torso and thin waistline that flared outward to form the wider hips and thighs that sat atop boney calf legs and bonier ankles.

"Aten has made these parts and they are beautiful at his hands," said the king.

"Yes, my king, but the art is no mirror of yourself but a mockery perhaps," said the queen.

"Then I shall be ridiculed for the sake of Aten."

"But we must be displayed with perfection for the sake of the monarchy and for the sake of our children and our children's children," the queen said.

"There is no part of my body that is not part of some god. My hair, although it is of wool, is the hair of Nu. My face, which is black, is the face of Ra."

Later that evening, at the king's house, he read to the queen the hymn to Osiris within the Papyrus of Ani. Although she came to understand the king's art, she struggled to understand the king's paradox. While he struggled to make one god in the land of plenty, it was this myriad of gods, which empowered him thorough their respective attributes, as symbolized by the new art, to defeat the established polytheism.

Chapter **9**

WATCHTOWERS

FROM THE watchtowers, forty feet above the Amarna city, soldiers surveyed the land for intruders, invaders, even foreigners seeking to have audience with the king. There were a multiplicity of watchtowers, stationed upon the ramparts at one-mile intervals, with panoramic views of the mountain on the east, the Nile on the west and the steles at the north and south borders. Whenever the sentries on the watchtowers discovered an eminent threat of invasion, their war horns would permeate Amarna, sending birds to flight and alarming the military to prepare for battle.

At present, the horns welcome through the gates of the city, foreign dignitaries by invitation of the king, to attend a special military ceremony. After a long procession, the foreign dignitaries joined the king and queen at the ceremonial pavilion, which along with the most important buildings of the monarchy stood on the processional avenue known as King's Way. The king's private house, olive grove, royal palace, Aten temple, bureaucratic buildings, ceremonial pavilion and the stepped terraces to the necropolis, were all accessible along the main avenue.

A full garrison of soldiers, charioteers and Nubian bowmen, conducted their military drills before the king, the queen, the court, the harem and all of the nobles and foreign dignitaries. It was a message to all in attendance that the new capital city of Amarna stood fortified with military power and it was the purpose of the king to convey it as such.

Of course, a few chosen ones from the Amen priest class at Thebes were invited, no doubt to remind them that the king was in full command of his army and able to fend of any potential invaders into the new capital— foreign or domestic.

Charioteers displayed their keen command of the horses, as they roared up and down the avenue in precise formation. While Nubian bowman struck copper targets with their arrows from a distance of fifty yards or more, Nubians skilled in the art of wrestling conducted imposing hand-to-hand drills.

Along the watchtowers, near the end of the ceremony, soldiers sounded war horns in secession, around the entire perimeter of the city arousing those in attendance to applaud. After the ceremony, the king and queen led the attendees to the offering tables along the avenue until they reached the Aten holy place, where the royal couple entered alone.

The day had been a success, and later at the king's villa, the king honored Aye, his military captain for an exquisite display of military strength and precision.

"Amarna is well protected under the watchful eye of my general," said the king. Yet, later upon the terrace, the king voiced some concerns to Ipy and Aye.

"The war horns were most impressive along the watchtowers, but I'm concerned about the sentries on guard as intruders could bribe the royal gatekeepers," said the king.

"Not to worry my king, I handpicked the sentries myself and they are the best and most trusted of all my soldiers," said Aye.

"How about the Nubian bowmen, they would make excellent sentries upon the watchtowers with their bows," said the king.

"The Nubians have their duties my king but they are foreigners—conscripted into the monarchy," said Aye, "but the loyalty of my trusted soldiers is abundant as they protect the Aten temples throughout the land."

The king, because he was reluctant to dampen Aye's upbeat spirit and successful day conveyed to him that his concerns were at rest, although it was contrary to what he felt.

"We are in good hands Ipy under the military command of our general," said the king.

"Yes my king," said Ipy

△△△

The actions of the monarchy in the ensuing days would test the presumed loyalty of Aye's military on their task to guard the workers that were sent to chisel away images of the gods throughout the land, even in their own childhood villages. The king's intent was to promote the sole and universal Aten over the tribal, village and local gods.

The new capital Amarna was prosperous from tax collections and trading in gold and jewels and with full granaries, the people were nourished and content. Peace prevailed and the threat and attempt on the king's life faded into the past.

Over time, however, while the monarchy's focus was on the administration of Amarna, the rest of the land fell into neglect. On the one hand, when it concerned Aten, Akhenaten wanted to avoid tribalism at all cost. On the other hand, with his favoritism of Amarna and neglect of the rest of Egypt, he was creating the tribalism, which he so despised.

The roads, buildings and open spaces outside of the new capital had overgrown with weeds. The holy places, buildings and monuments, built for eternity, fell into disrepair. The focus of the king was concentrated on the sole god, rather than the unity of the land, which had always been the strength of Egypt, and was something his father Amenhotep, knew well.

△△△

One night from the watchtowers, the sentries heard a strange, deafening noise that caused them to sound their war horns, which set into action the military garrison. There was confusion during the night but the next day the strange noise became obvious from the point of view of the watchtowers. A plague of locusts descended on the whole of Egypt, like ominous thunderclouds, devouring food crops and leaving a pillaged land in their wake.

All of a sudden, Amarna was a prosperous island in the midst of devastation and hunger. The loyal worshippers thought the prosperity was a blessing from Aten, although Aye sensed something more foreboding—more curse than a blessing.

The circumstances of poverty and looming starvation could cause the precarious balance between the old orthodoxy and the Aten worshipers of the monarchy to evaporate into thin air. More and more disquiet penetrated the ranks of the soldiers and diffused among the public, including the nobles whose crops were devastated. At the royal palace, some of the nobles waited in a reception room to have audience with the king—also attending were Ipy and Aye.

"Dear king, said the noble, the stockpiles of grain in the granaries will soon deplete. It is a most dire circumstance, calling for provisions from his majesty."

"Is it not the responsibility of the farmer to provide for his own subsistence during dire times as it is during times of plenty?" asked the king.

"The plague of locusts were not the fault of the farmers my king, your father provided for the hungry but your soldiers guard the granaries throughout the land, even those that are near depletion," said the noble.

"I shall order the soldiers to provide provisions to the nobles, and the nobles in turn, will give the food to the hungry and to the peasantry without compensation," said the king.

Throughout the day and into night, the nobles voiced their grievances and concerns, but the distress and ill-treatment of the defrocked priests, uncompensated soldiers, hungry commoners and starving peasants were unheard. And after the petitioners had left the palace, Aye, Ipy and the royal couple remained inside the throne room.

"Dear king, I am most concerned that the opening of the granaries will not be enough to quell the disquiet among the populace," said Aye.

"Aten will provide for them and restore *maat* to the land of Egypt," said the king

"Forgive me my lord, but did not Aten allow the hungry locusts to feed upon the food crops?" asked Aye.

"They have felt the power of the Aten, now they shall come to worship him," said Nefertiti.

Aye did not appreciate the comments of Nefertiti as he was attempting to inform the king about the need to restore balance, so he walked to the golden chalice and held it up in front of the throne.

"You remind us of the taster's demise," said Ipy.

"It should never be forgotten scribe. You should record it with your handy Tools of Thoth," said Aye.

"The Pharaoh-god is unperfected unlike the Aten, but I shall always strive for perfection like the bluest river, majestic mountains and golden barley fields and like all things made of Aten's hands. Never underestimate the power of your king, Aye, as I am the Pharaoh-god, and you are the general of the military by my appointment," said the king.

It was another display of the king's fatal flaw of stubbornness, to which Nefertiti was blind. She ran interference around any effort by Aye to persuade the king in her presence. Aye's interpretation of her meddling was that she was enabling the king to continue with his shortcomings and his stubborn persona.

Aye realized however that Ipy, having had a special relationship with the king as his childhood friend and fellow neophyte at the Amen temple, could get through to the king. Although Aye was general of the military and the king's uncle he had lost the ability to do so himself. He knew he had to confer with Ipy as soon as he could do so in private.

△△△

Meanwhile, the nobles had reneged on their promise to distribute food to the commoners and peasants because their own stockpiles were depleting. The disquiet among the hungry grew louder as time went on but their voices were still unheard by the monarchy. The Amen priests exploited the situation with the use of their own gold left over from the glory days, to bribe soldiers to unlock the granaries or to purchase food stockpiles from nobles and distribute it to the commoners and peasants.

Due to the dire circumstances, a resurgent enemy alliance between the peasants, priests, commoners and a few military men had taken place—unbeknownst to the king; but Aye had heard about it through his soldiers. So when Aye along with Ipy were sent by the king with a contingent of bureaucrats to the Nilometer, to measure the river in order to predict the proper tax assessment for the coming year's harvest, the two were able to converse about it in private.

"Royal scribe, the priests are at it again. They have exploited the situation of the famine, trading gold with the nobles in exchange for food for the hungry commoners and peasants," said Aye.

Leaving out the bribing of his soldiers for fear that the king may dismiss him from his post as general of the military.

"The nobles were instructed to go uncompensated for the provisions of food. Now their actions will diminish the image of the king in favor of the priests," said Ipy, "I shall inform the king at once."

"Scribe, because you have a special ear with the king, you must persuade him to appease the populace and relieve their causes of distress," said Aye, "we must redistribute the grain and gold to the masses and reopen the shuttered holy places."

"But general, you are the uncle to the king, the great uncle of Tutankhaten and brother to

Queen Tiye. The king treasures your advice, he told me himself," said Ipy.

"Yes, but Nefertiti's advise is treasured more, and we should have audience with the king together without the presence of her," said Aye.

"After the third day of the fasting each month, Meryaten and Meketaten always go along with their mother to collect olives in the grove, we will meet with the king then," said Ipy.

"Very well," said Aye.

Chapter **10**

PHARAOH-GOD

ON THE FIRST three days of each month, the royal family and all the people in the land of Egypt fasted and consumed emetic inducing herbs for cleansing. It had been a long established tradition since the time of the royal physician Imhotep.

As Ipy and Aye had discussed at the Nilometer, on the fourth day of each month, after the fasting, Queen Nefertiti did in fact walk to the grove with her daughters Meryaten and Meketaten to gather olives, which were favorite fruits of the king. Just as they arrived, a roar of thunder caused the girls to gather the olives in haste and drop the fruit on the ground. In anticipation of the rain and of playing their favorite hiding game with their mother, the girls were in a hurry to finish their chore.

It was the perfect place for hide-and-seek, with many places to conceal away within the uncultivated grove. Bushes grew underneath the canopy of the olive grove beside moss covered boulders, which tumbled down countless years ago from the nearby mountain and scattered themselves about here and there.

Meanwhile, Aye and Ipy went to the palace and waited inside the throne room to meet with the king who still had faith in Aye's soldiers and believed that things were returning to normal after the onslaught of locusts.

"Two of my most loyal and trusted servants, my general and my scribe, for what purpose have you desired this meeting?" asked the king.

"There is some news of which we must inform the king," said Ipy

"Why such a formal setting Ipy, are you petitioning me as the nobles to alleviate some grievance or another?" asked the king.

"No my king, said Ipy, "it's the gravity of the matter my king."

As Aye began to speak, the king interrupted,

"It is my old enemies yet again stirring up strife—bribing soldiers with gold to open the granaries and trading that same gold with the nobles to feed the commoners and peasants," said the king.

"How did you know?" Aye asked.

"The king has lots of eyes, my general, and an old friend among the priests who looked after me while I was in the hornet's nest—the Amen temple. I have the names of the bribed soldiers and the nobles who reneged on their promise," said the king.

"But the damage has been done," said Ipy, to the surprise of Aye, "the image of the king has diminished in favor of the priests among the commoners and peasants."

"With the defection of the traitors, the military ranks will grow even stronger, do you agree general?" asked the king.

"There could be a resurgence of the old alliance that formed just before our move to Amarna," said Aye.

"If the commoners and peasants combine with the priest class, it could mean trouble for the monarchy," said Ipy.

"Shall we hold audience for the petitions of thousands of commoners and peasants here in the throne room against royal protocol?" The king asked.

"We could reopen a few shuttered temples to appease the peasants and commoners," said Ipy, "and perhaps distribute some gold among the villages to share in the wealth of the kingdom."

"I shall quell any rebellion with our military," said the king.

"For now, I have command of the military, but the bribed soldiers give me cause for concern, my king," said Aye.

"I have expected that would be a concern one day general. I have conscripted thousands more Nubian bowmen—the finest in the world. Since the Pharaoh-god and son of Aten can never be defeated, my general and royal scribe should rest assured. Now how about a game of senet?" asked the king.

They retired to another room in the palace to drink beer and play senet, but with that diatribe, a second fatal flaw of the king had resurfaced—arrogance. The trait grew stronger with the relocation to the new capital perhaps, where he lived up to his self-titled position as king, prophet, and Pharaoh-god.

Aye detested the arrogance of the king more than his stubbornness, because the two together made for a comportment into which he could penetrate with rarity. Each time a meeting had ended with the king, Aye was left wanting. There was a desire in Aye to lecture the king but that was never an option, for the subordination of the uncle to his own nephew was a hindrance.

Aye had one last recourse. Because he knew the king's mother would instruct her son as to his administrative neglect and about the fine art of political appeasement, he consulted Queen Tiye.

△△△

During the hiding game, Nefertiti held in the wind her silver sistrum, which along with her singing, produced a musical tone the girls used to approximate the distance between their hiding place and their mother.

"Meryaten, Meketaten, where are you? I'm getting closer," Nefertiti sang.

Their mother's singing and the sound of the sistrum built up excitement for the girls, but on that day, unlike other days, the music and singing had become more than feint, it had become silent and drowned out by the louder and more frequent thunder and the rain which began to downpour. When it seemed the girls would remain undiscovered by their mother in their hiding places, they came into the open and called out to her.

The game and the fun were over, and the sternness and unhappiness in the weather warned of something foreboding. Their calls went unanswered though, and their mother appeared to be hiding from them, although this was something she had never done before.

As time went on their search became sobering and then fearfulness set in when all of a sudden through the canopy of the olive grove overhead, they saw a pink mass of flamingoes taking flight under the gray sky. Something had driven them from the pond and the girls ran to discover what it was. As they reached the edge of the grove, at the southern most trees, they sighted in the distance, two chariots in flight away from the pond and out of the Amarna border. When the chariots disappeared, the girls hurried home to inform the king, but when they discovered that he was away, they told their younger brother Tutankhaten to summon their father.

The king was still at the royal palace with Aye and Ipy when Tutankhaten informed him of Nefertiti's disappearance. The senet game came to an abrupt ending as the king, Aye and Ipy returned Tutankhaten to the king's house. After speaking to the girls and posting sentries around the king's house, the king and Aye summoned three-hundred of his trusted soldiers and Nubian bowmen who sped their chariots to the olive grove.

On arrival, a soldier discovered a blood covered sistrum near the trunk of an olive tree near the edge of the grove and climbed the watchtower at the city boundary to question the sentries, but the two were missing along with their chariots. Although the evidence implicated the sentries, the king realized it was the work of his old enemies.

The king, Aye and the soldiers continued their trek south toward Thebes in search of Nefertiti, interrogating and searching every village and city along the way. No rock was unturned, no tree was unshaken, and no abode escaped a most thorough rummaging on the way to Thebes. But as the king and his soldiers went about the search for the queen in desperation, she was yet unfound.

As the sun began to set, and as all else had failed, the king concentrated on his enemies, the Amen priests, and dispatched his soldiers and Nubian bowman to set up camp and surround their temple complex throughout the night.

△△△

Ipy, distressed by the disappearance had searched alone for Nefertiti throughout the day and arrived at the somber campsite during the night to console the king.

"We shall find her my king I assure you," said Ipy, but the king was already resigned to the fate of Nefertiti.

"When Tutankhaten informed me of the news, I am convinced by his resigned behavior that he already knew of his mother's death, as the divine seer has always been within the child," said the king.

"It is true my king, the young spirits of children tend to be clairvoyant, but perhaps it was melancholy that produced the boy's behavior," said Ipy.

"After he informed me, he stood silent for a moment, staring with intensity at nothing in particular. Then, after nodding his head, as if to a thing he was told, he said in a boy's voice, that his mother was among the venerable ones," said the king.

"Yes, I heard it as well my king, but no doubt tomorrow we shall locate her in Thebes," said Ipy.

"If the queen is with the venerable ones reaping the golden wheat in the field of peace, tomorrow I shall avenge her death."

As dawn ushered in the next day, Aye and thirty of his soldiers departed from the temple of Amen and continued their search for Nefertiti. The night before, the king and Ipy had left the camp, and visited the nearby royal house of Queen Tiye in Thebes and stayed there overnight.

The king informed her of the circumstances of Nefertiti's disappearance, and gave orders for his Nubian bowman instead of Egyptian soldiers to escort her to the king's house in Amarna to join her grandchildren.

After seven days, when the location of Nefertiti was still unknown, the king took as his prisoners, four priests from their homes and the two sentries who abandoned their posts at the watchtower. And after completing a somber ritual of shaving and cleansing, the king entered the Amen temple and took for his prisoners four priests inside. One of them was the uncle of Senen.

In a sheep's pen on the other side of the city, Aye tied the captives together and interrogated them throughout the remainder of the day and night to no avail.

Meanwhile outside of the temple, the king made a proclamation, which Ipy recorded into the stele at the pylons.

"I shaved and bathed in the sacred lake and adorned fine white linen before entering the temple to smite the enemies of the son of Aten. The seedling of the prince in his mother's womb was their enemy and they tried to kill him. They conspired with the queen's harem to kill the king but killed the royal taster. The enemies of Aten caused to disappear, the Lady of the Two Plumes, the Queen Mother who ruled over the two lands, the royal wife and chief wife of the king, Nefertiti. They stole her away from her children in the olive grove on the day of thunder, and they will meet their end by stake above the waters of the Nile and watchful eyes of crocodiles," proclaimed the king.

The next day, summoned to the occasion of the impalements of her uncle and seven other Amen priests and two soldiers, was Senen along with nobles, commoners and peasants.

The screams of the captives rolled like river torrents, while the agonizing stakes of wood punctured and impaled them one by one. As blood flowed and as dusk arrived, the Nubian bowman planted the stakes in the river facing east toward Aten's morning rise, above the snapping jaws of crocodiles, and below flying things picking at the flesh. The impalements, ten of them, cast brilliant silhouettes against the blood-orange sun setting in the western horizon.

Chapter **11**

ABDICATION

AFTER PUTTING to death the ten Egyptians, which were his own fellow citizens, and casting out Senen who became a beggar, the king returned to Amarna. Now the king had become one with the beggar, it seemed, as his Pharaoh-god stature diminished with his derelict duty to uphold *maat*—the balance, peace and harmony of the land and its people.

Amarna was prosperous while the effect of the locusts on the rest of Egypt was like a million shepherds grazing sheep in the crop fields. As starvation began to set in, the king had fewer eyes among the people and more enemies bent on revenge, so it was necessary to conscript more Nubian bowman for good measure. After all, the king's trust in his own soldiers diminished due to the disappearance of Nefertiti.

Soldiers, tiring of the lack of compensation for their services began looting shuttered holy places and necropolis tombs for hidden treasures, and deserting their posts in droves. Yet the most ominous sign of trouble to come was a meeting between those soldiers and the commoners and peasantry, without the nobles and priests. The alliance was one that was independent from the priests, although the priests were welcome to join; and symbolized the people's unity with the military and their political awakening.

It had been with certainty that this time would come—an accumulation of the king's neglect and faults of stubbornness and lack of appeasement had brought the populace to the brink. To hasten the inevitable rebellion, some among the vengeful set fire to the granaries to deplete the remaining stock. And General Aye's attempts to warn the stubborn king of such a dreadful scenario had been futile.

△△△

Aye called to assembly his entire military of charioteers, bowmen and soldiers as tension throughout the land continued to heighten. He intended to ferret out any potential instigators of possible rebellion, but at the designated place and time of the meeting, as he waited without any loss of patience, a full third of his army failed to show. When the soldiers in attendance informed him that a military exercise was underway near the city of Elephantine, he hurried at once to contend with the deserters.

When Aye approached on his chariot to the edge of the field where the military deserters were gathered, he discovered there before his eyes some of his most brave, loyal and formidable soldiers. The leaders among them approached him.

"Our loyalty has depleted under the heretic that destroyed our temples and gods," said the leader.

"There are but a few of you, what do you propose to do?" asked Aye.

"Among us here, yes we are few, but there are others: commoners, peasants, priests and more of your soldiers assembled but unseen. They are more patient than we are but soon they too will join us. Our loyalty to the general remains strong but we will soon revolt if the gods and our compensation are not restored," said the leader.

"Remain you patient soldier, and I will see to it that the holy places are reopened and the gods and compensation restored. I shall speak with the king," said Aye.

Now it was apparent to Aye that the king and the entire Eighteenth Dynasty were facing rebellion by an alliance that consisted of his own soldiers, along with the commoners and peasants. Although he had been quite certain he could defeat them, perhaps with the help of Nubia, a staunch ally; such a battle would be fierce and prolonged, leaving the dynasty vulnerable and susceptible to foreign invasion. Since he wanted to avoid such a scenario at all costs, he sought a compromise instead. Still, he would need to convince a stubborn king that a compromise was necessary and imperative as the king's very life was in danger. If successful, there was the potential to conserve and increase his own power and stature among his soldiers and among the general populace.

When General Aye reached Amarna later that afternoon, the Nubian bowmen were conducting there own impressive drills from their chariots—piercing targets hoisted into the air at full gallop. Since the king had lots of eyes or spies, the Nubian drills per chance meant that the king had already planned to go to war and perhaps he had already alerted Nubia to join the battle.

This scenario could weaken Aye's powers of persuasion, so upon entering the king's house he was pleased that his sister, Queen Tiye, was present, as she had also admonished the king about his careless treatment of the ancient gods and temples.

"We must persuade the king my sister, for the life of the dynasty and the life of the king are in jeopardy," said Aye.

"What is the matter my brother, with your army, you are the most powerful man in Egypt next to the king," said Tiye.

"You shall here it when I tell it to the king," said Aye.

"He is on the terrace with Ipy the scribe," said Tiye.

Upon the terrace, the king and Ipy observed the Nubians practicing their military drills on a field in the distance as Aye joined them with Queen Tiye.

"The Nubians are the best bowmen in the world, Aye," said the king.

"Agreed, my king, but there are too few to stop the rebel alliance against the monarchy," said Aye.

"I have heard from you before, Aye, about this alliance and it was of no concern then or now," said the king.

"Yes my king," said Aye, "but half of my soldiers are aligned with priests, commoners and even peasants to overthrow the monarchy. Your life is in danger my king."

"We shall call upon our Nubian allies at once," said the king.

"That could mean a prolonged war, the dynasty could be weakened, and made vulnerable to foreign invasion, perhaps even the Nubians would turn on us. Compromise would be the wiser course of action, my king," said Aye.

"Compromise you say, on what matter?" The king asked.

"The holy places could be reopened and the gods restored beside the Aten," said Aye, "and the soldiers must be compensated so that they can support their families."

"Aten is the sole god in the land and his holy places shall remain open," said the king.

"A few reopened temples will not diminish the Aten, my son, perhaps you should reconsider restoring a few of the ancient gods," said Tiye.

"Never in a thousand million years will the imposter gods be restored; and never in a thousand million years will the temples reopen," said the king.

Inflexibility was what Aye expected of the stubborn king but now it was time to appeal to Queen Tiye, to convince the king to abdicate in favor of his heir, the ten-year-old Prince Tutankhaten, in order to preserve the dynasty. When the stubborn king turned his attention back to the Nubian bowmen, Aye spoke with the queen in privacy.

"The dynasty of our father's fathers will weaken and come to an end as the king is unwilling to compromise," said Aye, "you must convince him to go to Sinai to save the dynasty and to preserve his own life. He must abdicate the throne to the young prince." Tiye agreed and to her son, the king, she said,

"The dynasty and the monarchy we must preserve, and you must for a while go to Sinai and abdicate the throne to Tutankhaten. Appeasement is at times a necessity, a weapon even among royalty. Or would you rather take the chance that while at war with our Egyptian enemies, foreigners invade also, jeopardizing the monarchy and the lives of your daughters and your heir?"

During the ensuing days, after some long contemplation about foreign invasions and prospects of a long civil war, the king agreed that compromise was the wiser choice, and abdicated the throne in order to preserve the dynasty.

At the young age of ten years, Tutankhaten ascended the throne to become king along with his Great Uncle Aye as coregent. Once again, Queen Tiye persuaded her stubborn son to make the wiser choice as she had persuaded him to build the new capital Amarna way from his Theban enemies.

Chapter **12**

THE BOY KING

BECAUSE TUTANKHATEN at the age of ten was to become king, attendants bathed him in lime, and anointed him with the fat of a crocodile and scented oils. A coronation of a king was a time of celebration, but the coronation of the boy king was toned-down due to the circumstances of his father's abdication.

It was a defining moment for the people and for the land, since the dynasty was vulnerable during these times more than in recent history due to the political infighting between the orthodoxy and new monotheism resulting from Akhenaten's religious reforms.

Because of this internal strife, Queen Tiye was careful to invite the old priests from the shuttered holy places to the coronation. Since nobles and priests questioned whether the boy king would continue the policies of his father, Tiye sought to make the atmosphere conciliatory and pleasant, to disarm them of any malice toward the boy before he reached the throne.

Because foreigners often sensed weakness during times of transition in Egypt, royal messengers carried letters to leaders abroad, to remind them of Egypt's strength and readiness for battle, while Aye sent soldiers to reinforce the borders.

This was the political climate of infighting—the shuttered temples, expunged priests and outlawed gods, that set the stage for Tutankhaten's rule. And to the surprise and annoyance of Queen Tiye, the appeaser, and Aye, the mediator, King Tutankhaten did mimic his father's policies. This was due in part to his devotion to Aten but also to the letters sent from his father in the Sinai.

His father Akhenaten cast a large shadow over the kingdom, ruling in absentia, through his son. For whenever Queen Tiye, Aye or members of his court advised him on matters of importance, Tutankhaten, through letters or royal messengers, sought the consul of his father.

This continued for the first three years of his reign; but at the age of fourteen, in the course of his awakening, as he was frustrated with the dilapidated holy places and monuments left by his father, Tutankhaten explored his own soul for guidance.

ΔΔΔ

With a physical presence and face to behold, Tutankhaten did live up to the meaning of his name—the living image of the lord—and it was a name his father gave to him before his birth into royalty. The kings of Nubia, Libya and Syria came to see with their own eyes, the baby that was born like a blossom from a lotus.

The young king, to legitimize his place as heir, took for his wife, his royal half-sister, Ankhsenpa-aten, but sorrow would come of their effort to produce an heir. Ankhsenpa-aten, during her seventh month of pregnancy came into labor inside the nursery of the royal palace. After thirteen hours, a physician delivered the baby—a girl devoid of oxygen and life. This sorrowful event followed two years later with the stillbirth of another baby girl.

The young king fell into despair and went away for days at a time upon his silver chariot accompanied by his soldiers away from the royal palace. He seemed to assume the role of his father, traveling throughout the land and with his own eyes witnessing the damage to the temples, which his father shuttered. He saw them and they were dilapidated and devoid of life with crumbling walls and floors and strangling weeds that crept over tables, chairs and alters.

The soldiers began to worry about the king's behavior, for inside the various cities and villages scattered between the temples, the boy king of habit dismounted his chariot and walked among the people. This was odd enough for a king, but he also entered their houses to chat with them for a time. He seemed to be searching and stared long into the eyes of each woman he met. Each time after his search and without a word, he climbed onto his chariot and led his soldiers to the next holy place or city along the way.

When the king and his contingent arrived at a village one day, which was not very far from Amarna, it would have been their last stop before returning to the royal palace nearby. The commoners as always lay bowed before him when he would enter their homes and walk with them along the pathways. After entering all the homes in the village and greeting every woman and child, he happened across a beggar as he stepped onto his chariot. She reached for his arm first and then his leg and grabbed it before a soldier's reprimand.

"Leave her be," said the Tutankhaten. The beggar girl washed the dust off his foot after removing his sandal and stood high upon her knees to whisper to the king.

"You are searching for your mother, Nefertiti," said the beggar, "I know where you can find her."

The king quieted her whisper, and stood her up.

"What say you?" asked the king.

"You will find her in the yellow mountain, inside a cave," said the beggar.

Shocked by what he had heard, the king looked toward the yellow mountain, which bordered Amarna, with astonishment, and gathered the beggar girl onto his chariot. In a manner befitting royalty, he raised his sword toward Amarna and returned to the palace.

ΔΔΔ

Inside the palace, Ankhsenpa-aten's harem laughed at the beggar girl for displaying her foul clothes and foul manners.

"Silence, for you may trade places with her and become beggars," said the king, "Bathe her and deliver her to the servant's sleeping room," said Ankhsenpa-aten.

"Then perfume her and dress her in fine linen befitting a harem girl," said the king.

"Do no such thing unless the king wishes to have his own harem," said Queen Ankhsenpa-aten.

"No," interjected the beggar girl, "I mean, with all do respect my king, I cannot accept such a charitable gesture, as I am unworthy," said the beggar.

Unworthy especially of the royal treatment as her hair was matted and the dirt upon her face formed a mask. In spite of that, and although her fingernails and toenails were long arsenal, she carried with her a charm and attitude which contradicted the reality of her stature.

"You are among the queen's harem," said the king.

When the harem girls escorted the beggar to the bathing room, Ti, a brooding but curious harem girl, who hoped to become a second wife of the king, followed close behind them. When they undressed her, Ti's fret became concern, for what she saw was a body that men imagine in their dreams.

She stared now at the grime on her face and expected no difference in the look of it behind that mask of dirt but her face was as her body, a dream of men, and seeing it, Ti dashed out of the bathing room.

△△△

The next day, King Tutankhamen and Aye set out for the yellow mountain, which overlooked Aten city, for he had informed Aye about his encounter with the beggar. After reaching the foot of the mountain, they hiked up a slope, gripping and pulling the parched grass until reaching a cave.

Tutankhamen waited outside as Aye searched the darkness inside the cave where particles of dust danced in the scattered rays of sunlight. The scattered light revealed bats hanging from the ceiling and in close proximity to them a body of a woman, which he recognized to be Nefertiti as it adorned a queen's royal tunic. The climate inside the cave conserved the body of the queen for the most part yet the flesh that revealed patches of bone trifled with the afterlife.

Aye removed the gold and silver bracelets on her wrists and rings from her fingers and a scarab necklace, and with his knife, cut braids from the head of the queen and presented it to Tutankhaten. While sitting there, the king looked at what he held—the braids and jewelry—and gathered into his nostrils the fragrance of perfume that lingered long after the occasion of her death. Aye watched him in his sorrow and wondered would he repeat the actions of his father; recalling the silhouettes of the impaled bodies over the Nile against the backdrop of the setting sun, and the unrest that followed.

The king stumbled as they descended the mountain before Aye held his hand sensing his weakness from grief. After slipping again descending the mountain, Tutankhaten sat for a moment overlooking Amarna.

"There are things unaccomplished by my father," said Tutankhaten, "there are loose ends that must be tied together...and yet there are things that must be undone."

"What do you mean my king?" asked Aye.

"He shuttered the holy places and they have become eye soars to Aten, neglected and dilapidated. He murdered the priests who stole away Nefertiti, but never found her to give her proper burial. And in his zeal to make Aten the singular god of the universe, he succeeded in making him tribal...the god of a few in Egypt and the few exiled in the Sinai," said Tutankhaten.

"Yes, I understand my king."

Aye, pleased at what he had heard from the young king—distancing himself from his father, placed the hands of Tutankhaten upon his shoulders the rest of the way down the yellow mountain.

ΔΔΔ

Despite the terrible condition of the semi-decomposed remains of her body, Nefertiti was mummified. Embalmers embalmed her body and wrapped it in fine linen held fast together with perfumed resin. Around and around the head, torso, arms, hands, legs, each finger and each toe hundreds of times with precise folds according to the protocol of royalty.

After seventy days of official mourning, King Tutankhaten as a priest of the highest rank officiated over his mother's funerary ritual, wearing a special white tunic for the occasion. The head of an embroidered ankh formed the neck of the tunic, and the remainder part of the ankh, the cross, extended past the waistline. Ostrich plumes surrounded the queen's coffin as the king spoke.

"Nefertiti germinates again and springs forth like the lotus blossom; she comes to life and lives again among the godlike ones in the fields of peace."

After the funerary sacrament, embalmers placed the queen's coffin inside a silver sarcophagus and entombed her in the Valley of the Queens.

ΔΔΔ

After the queen's burial, the royal family dispersed bread and beer throughout Egypt and held a feast at the royal palace to celebrate her afterlife. Dignitaries and nobles from near and far came to celebrate the lost queen.

"The god of life; the lord of love and peace; the emerald light and president of the mountains; receive Nefertiti, the beautiful one, Queen Mother of the two lands and royal wife, into the field of peace; a place of beauty of splendor and of lotuses; among the venerable ones," said Tutankhaten.

After Tutankhaten began the occasion with those brief words, he joined the Queen of Nubia, his grandmother Tiye, Aye, royal wife, Ankhsenpa-aten and sisters Meryaten and Meketaten at a banquet table.

Meryaten and Meketaten were silent in their grief, in between audible sobs, for they still felt the shock from the lost of their mother and had hoped to one day find her alive. Their Great Uncle Aye reminisced about the lost queen and told a tender story of how she loved to dance and play the sistrum and the hide-and-seek game with the girls.

This atmosphere around the table became more jovial, even Meryaten and Meketaten managed to smile at the stories their great uncle recalled about their mother. Then Queen Tiye clapped her hands and gestured to the servants.

"More honey wine," she said.

The beggar girl with the attractive looks and pleasing body approached Queen Tiye from behind and poured wine into her golden chalice. As she continued serving around the table, the beggar spoke, which surprised everyone for servants were to serve and never to speak.

"My queen, do you not recognize me? It is me Senen, a girl of the harem."

Senen spoke as the queen took her first sip of wine from the chalice, and because of what the queen had heard, let the wine flow out of her mouth and back into the fancy cup—a royal spit. From the table she gathered a linen napkin and soaked the residual wine from her lips—and as discreet as she could, behind the cover of the napkin—also from her tongue.

As always, the removal of the crown from her head preceded the queen's abandonment of royal comportment. And as if on cue, the servants removed Meryaten and Meketaten to their sleeping room before the queen had spoken.

"Senen was sent away as an outcast, why is she here in the presence of the king?" she asked Tutankhaten.

"She is no outcast," said Tutankhaten.
The king ordered Senen to sit at the table with the royal family and to the astonishment of everyone in attendance, the king served Senen food to eat and honey wine to drink.

"Do you know who she is?" asked Queen Tiye.

"Yes I know," said the king, "I know that she was questioned about the unfortunate death of the royal taster."

"My queen, I was never found guilty of killing the royal taster," said Senen.

"Silence, King Akhenaten spared you for his own reasons but not your uncle the priest; how did you know the whereabouts of Nefertiti?" asked Queen Tiye.

"When his majesty sent me away from Amarna, I discovered a place to sleep inside a cave in the foothills of the Yellow Mountain. One day after the queen went missing; I returned to the cave and discovered her body," said Senen.

"Nefertiti would be without proper burial had it not been for Senen," said Tutankhaten, "for that, I forgave all her transgressions." Then he spoke to Senen.

"If you wish to reach the place of beauty and splendor and of lotuses in the field of peace among the venerable ones, one day— you must separate yourself from sin."

"Yes my king," said Senen, bowing her way out of the room.

ΔΔΔ

After messengers returned from the Sinai, to report on the conditions of the exiles, the king was unpleased. After receiving the news of their suffering and the terrible behavior of the shepherds and strangers that accompanied Akhenaten and the priests in exile, King Tutankhaten decided to visit Sinai.

Upon his arrival, he found the people to be suffering from all sorts of illness including various skin conditions that caused itching and rashes to spread among them. Shouting and fighting was rampant and as routine as the thievery of milk and bread from the mothers and their infants. Although there was a well nearby and an oasis of vegetation and sheep and fish from the sea, some of them who were lazy and greedy stole to get their fill.

Because the conditions in the camp were desolate, the king conferred with Akhenaten inside the tabernacle tent at the foot of Mount Sinai, and while doing so, heard and seen the disruptive behavior of the outcast shepherds and polluted ones for himself.

"These people are disobedient and in need of the palace law," said Tutankhaten.

"As you know, the shepherds were never a refined people. They once burned corpses on the campfire where they also cooked the meat of a lamb," said Akhenaten, "one man robbed another who murdered him in return for the crime."

"The confessions of the dead in the Papyrus of Ani are also for the living, to live in peace according to law and separate themselves from sin," said Tutankhaten.

Akhenaten agreed, because he was also frustrated with the behavior of his followers. He and Tutankhaten recorded on gesso tablets the laws that were familiar to the priests but unfamiliar to the majority of the multitude.

I have not done iniquity
I have not robbed with violence
I have not stolen
I have done no murder
I have not defrauded offerings
I have not diminished oblations
I have not plundered the god
I have spoken no lies
I have not snatched away food
I have not caused pain
I have not committed fornication
I have not caused shedding of tears
I have not dealt in deceit
I have not transgressed
I have not acted with guile
I have not laid waste the plowed land
I have not been an eavesdropper
I have not set my lips in motion against others
I have not been angry except for a just cause
I have not defiled the wife of any man
I have not polluted myself
I have not caused terror

I have not burned with rage
I have not turned any away from right and truth
I have not worked grief
I have not acted with insolence
I have not stirred up strife
I have not judged in haste
I have not multiplied my words exceedingly
I have done neither harm nor ill.

ΔΔΔ

Soon after administering the laws to the people, Tutankhaten returned to Egypt after giving assurance to Akhenaten that the absent king's affairs would continue. Although upon his return, he presided over a jubilee celebrating his fifth year reign and invited even the defrocked Amen priests to attend, which was against his father's wishes.

During the jubilee, the king announced the changing of his name to Tutankhamen, which was a surprise to those in attendance. For the changing of the king's name was symbolic of the restoral of Amen and other gods and the gesture made the king an adoring figure beloved by the people.

Yet Tutankhamen remained loyal to Aten in secret and used the gods as appeasers to draw the people nearer to his Aten. The king viewed Aten as a universal god for all the people, rather than a god for a few tribal heretics, shepherds and outcasts. The king realized that localized tribalism was a perversion of monotheism and diminishment of Aten.

The king's political appeasement at the jubilee returned *maat*—a renewed sense of balance, reciprocity and peace to Egypt; and the restoral of it, by Tutankhamen—the peacemaker was witnessed by the people and retold countless times in every city and village. He had made his mark, for the restoral of peace to the land was his calling and peacemakers are the blessed ones of Aten. Now he was beloved by all the people— nobles, peasants and even the military.

Two years after his fifth jubilee, restoral of the gods and peace throughout the land remained and worshippers of all gods coexisted in peace. Yet, the continued suffering of Akhenaten and his followers exiled in the Sinai troubled Tutankhamen so much that he dispatched the following letter to his father, the exiled King Akhenaten.

Akhenaten, as the eldest son of Aten in heaven, through my royal and divine birth, and the living image of him, I was unpleased with the conditions of the holy places and monuments, even as you were once unpleased before me. I undertook the beautification of the temples and monuments, which will please the Aten, my father in heaven. I restored peace in the land of Egypt among the people. I restored the expunged gods of the dilapidated sanctuaries and the people will worship them along side the Aten. This is for the sake of peace and the restoration of balance and reciprocity that we call maat, and for Aten, who blesses the peacemakers. Akhenaten, you and the priests of Aten and the loyal followers of Aten there with you in exile may return to Egypt and live in peace among your neighbors and even among your enemies. No harm will come to you, as I am the powerful son and living image of the lord.

Akhenaten was unpleased by his son Tutankhaten's letter, although it reminded him of the conversation he once had with his own father concerning those very same monuments. It also reminded him of just how far he himself had wondered away from his role as overseer of temples. Although he felt he was right to close the temples and to expunge the gods, he also neglected to maintain them.

The letter, he worried, could represent the boy king's coming of age and independence from his father at fourteen years of age, that perhaps he would begin making decisions separate from his father who had been to this time, governing in absentia. While in exile, Akhenaten had remained in charge all along.

Even after the abdication, his royal court remained loyal, as did Queen Tiye and his general of the military, Aye.

But when this news of the restoral of the gods and of the Amen priests and the name change of Tutankhamen reached the Sinai, there was much displeasure for many interpreted the actions of the young king as not just an innocent coming of age, but blasphemous. And because of this and because Akhenaten no longer ruled in absentia, for his son had undone the laws, which he implemented; this compelled him to return a letter to Tutankhamen.

You are the administrator of the king's affairs while he is absent, but now just your affairs concern you. With the return of the gods and the Amen priests, and the removal of Aten from your name, those here see you as a traitor and blasphemer. What is the truth what is thy motive?

Through peaceful means and concession, Tutankhamen succeeded in making Aten universal rather than tribal and attracted some new converts over. Of course, the reopened holy places and full granaries appeased the public and made them consider for the first time, the possibility of worshipping Aten. This was his motivation, and he knew that

Akhenaten would understand this if he and his exiles returned to Egypt to live in peace among their neighbors.

This motivated him also to take six of his soldiers with him to Sinai a second time to convince Akhenaten and his followers to return to Egypt. As he traveled, he had a determination to put the record straight and his intent was to silence for the last time any charge of blasphemy against him and convince the exiles to return to Egypt and live in peace. Yet because the people harbored ill will towards him and because of their stubbornness, they could be reluctant to leave their oasis of desolation.

"They accuse the king of blasphemy," said Tutankhamen to himself as he rode his silver and gold chariot, "But I am the son of Aten a peacemaker and image of the lord."

After miles of travel, the king and his soldiers arrived and dismounted the chariots near the tented tabernacle at the foot of Mount Sinai. Inside the tent, Tutankhamen spoke with authority to Akhenaten and the high priests of Aten.

"Who shall speak? What is it then, this talk of blasphemy? Who dare accuse me? I have power over your mouths through the Aten, the lord of right and truth," said Tutankhamen.

"All of the affairs of the absent king are undone by you," said Akhenaten.

"Yes, the dilapidated temples overgrown with weeds are now returned to their worthy places," said Tutankhamen.

"Places to worship other gods?" asked a priest.

"Aten the unseen one is in every holy place my priest, the minor gods will convince the people to covet the supreme one."

After that exchange with Akhenaten and the priests, Tutankhamen came out of the tent to address the multitude assembled together as they noticed the king's chariot.

"*Maat*—love, peace, charity, harmony, balance, order and proportion is the right way and is restored in the people and in the land of Egypt. Peace is amongst the people and milk, honey, bread and melons are plentiful. The granaries are full with barley and wheat and there is plenty of fruit on the trees and plants harvesting. Return to Egypt and live in peace with your neighbors and you shall witness the restoral of *maat*: balance, fairness and peace," said Tutankhamen,

"In peace they all live, soldiers, nobles, commoners and even peasants together in Egypt. All you farmers come and cultivate the land. Artisans of all kinds, apply your trade. Physicians tend to the sick. Potters make pottery to carry water and food crops and shepherds herd your sheep in peace. The Aten is the chief and universal god."

"He is the only god," someone shouted.

"You have changed your name," said a shepherd.

"The *ka*, the spirit has no name. It joins you at birth to awaken you to consciousness, yet you wander here unconscious of the grandeur of life. Renew your spirits and ascend the latter of change," said Tutankhamen.

"Renew your name and the old gods and temples," said another.

"My name and the restored gods were necessary appeasements to return *maat* to the people of Egypt for appeasement is necessary for peace and peacemakers are blessings from Aten," Tutankhamen said.

The talk about appeasement agitated the crowd who pointed blame at the king, but Akhenaten and his priests remained silent, never coming to the king's defense. The wind stirred the clouds and the bright tunic of the king, which gleamed in comparison to the scruffiness of the horde and dusk of day.

"Traitor," someone shouted.

The soldiers shielded the king.

"Yes, the blasphemer," shouted another.

The crowd pushed against the soldiers and a murmur resonated like the drone of a hornet's nest when a soldier tried to remove his sword. Two shepherds attacked the soldier with their crooks and the rest attacked the remaining soldiers like a swarm of hornets.

"Stop, I command you for I am the Pharaoh god," said Tutankhamen, but the multitude had no consideration for his authority.

"The Pharaoh god of Amen," someone shouted.

"King of the Amenists," accused another.

When a man reached for the king, the crowd appeared to stop him, but it was the crowd pulling at one another to reach the king also. They yanked him in every direction—all four limbs with such force that it separated his hip and shoulder joints and fractured his clavicle and femur bones.

Akhenaten and the priests observed the onslaught at the start without interference, but as Tutankhamen cried out in agony, from the torture, a priest put a stop to it. Perhaps it was compassion or the penalty of blasphemy that compelled the priest to tie a rope around the neck of the king and hang him from a sycamore tree. As he swayed there back and forth and as the night fell, the silent crowd stood there staring at what they had done. Tutankhamen's soldiers who were no match for the aggression escaped and returned to Egypt to inform Aye of the king's death.

Chapter **13**

OPENING OF THE MOUTH

THE NEXT WEEK Aye the coregent ascended the throne to continue the Eighteenth Dynasty since King Tutankhamen died without an heir. With an eye towards vengeance, Aye and his soldiers numbering in the hundreds, traveled with quickness to Sinai to claim the body of the beloved young king.

It was Aye's intent to avenge the murder of the king after the seventy-day period of official mourning and mummification, but upon reaching Sinai, before speaking a word, he and his soldiers put to death ten exiles and hung them before approaching Akhenaten.

"You stood and witnessed your son the peacemaker tortured and murdered," said Aye.

"Even my son, even for a king the penalty for blaspheming the Aten is death," said Akhenaten.

"The king made Aten a god of gods subservient to none and beloved by more and more people each day; for Aten was present during the restoral of the temples and the lesser gods," said Aye, "You Akhenaten will see the error of your ways for there was no blasphemy in the king, but a devout love of the Aten."

△△△

During the mourning and mummification process, hundreds of artisans and scribes went about the task of preparing the young king for his resurrection into the afterlife. Embalmers wrapped fine linen, interlaced with a sweet smelling resin, in hundreds of layers around the body. A gilded shrine covered a jar containing the king's internal organs, and a solid-gold death mask, guarded his body and spirit. And just as in his sentient life, his two daughters, tiny mummies, were beside him again in the afterlife.

As embalmers were busy with their work in the mortuary, artisans prepared a sarcophagus made of pink quartzite for the king's entombment and sculpted a solid gold coffin in the exact likeness of the king's face and suffering eyes. Each of the king's possessions occupied a nook or cranny within the tomb for the eternal journey: chariots, bows, swords, arrows, fine jewels, guardians, companions, thrones, wreaths of flowers and fruits, scepters of royalty, sandals, gloves and tunics.

And when the preparation for the king's burial was complete, the priests laid upon his chest the winged scarab of rebirth.

After the body of the king had been prepared and all of his belongings were in their places along with his beloved daughters, out of his mouth arose a spirit. The king's spirit stood before his wife Ankhsenpa-Aten, holding a silver ankh—the symbol of life—or in the case of a dead Pharaoh— a symbol of life after death.

Chapter **14**

FLIGHT

FOUR YEARS after Tutankhamen's burial, King Aye died a death of mystery without an heir to the throne and the mysterious death of Aye caused rumor to spread among the nobility and commoners.

Some believed the exiled Akhenaten even from the remote Sinai, somehow done away with Aye. After all, the former king had become weary of the Sinai wilderness and still believing the throne was his, had plans to return and rule. For after Tutankhamen restored the gods and holy places, Akhenaten was determined as ever to remove them and close them once again.

And Aten remained the sole god in his mind even after thirteen years in the Sinai. Even after Akhenaten's royal tunics made of fine linen became humble cloths and even after the clean shaved face of the exiled Pharaoh became a disobedient beard, he still praised Aten.

The terrain of Sinai was made of sand colored rocks speckled with occasional wild foliage, bushes and trees of green that formed sparse sanctuaries in the desolate peninsula situated east of Egypt between two arms of the Red Sea. The Egyptians refused to build any monuments or holy places there nor bridges or obelisks or even a necropolis. Sinai, the land of bushes, was a sparseness of civil structure apart from the Road of Horus built north near the Mediterranean. From it, there was access from Egypt east into the land of Palestine and beyond.

The Sinai was used as a military outpost—a strategic area to defend the border from marauding foreigners, and stage the military or to rest them after battle. The location of each outpost near water wells was convenient for a thirsty military.

On the southern part of the peninsula at the foot of a mountain also called Sinai, was a sparse sanctuary where Akhenaten and his priests first settled and built a tented tabernacle. In all, it was a desolate place to live but there was a perennial water source, a wellspring, which was unused by the soldiers as it was the southern most well on the Sinai Peninsula that sustained the oasis and the exiles.

Much of the land was infertile as sand and hostile to farming yet the perpetual source of water from the well sustained the oasis and quenched the thirst of the exiles. Cattle and sheep grazed on the wild vegetation and in turn nourished the exiles with their milk and meat, and fish were plentiful in the sea.

Still, Akhenaten the former king had no military command and the little gold they possessed was useless except for bartering sheep from roaming shepherds on occasion; some of whom, joined them at the sanctuary and brought with them their own ignorance and bad-manners.

In his desire to please Aten, he sacrificed the lost of his family: Nefertiti, Tutankhamen and Aye had all died; Queen Tiye and his daughters Meryaten and Meketaten were unseen for many years, although he heard from them through messengers and letters. The opulent confines of the royal palace were gone and so were the royal court and the admiration of the foreign diplomats, nobles, military and peasantry. It was he and his little tribe of exiled worshippers and those still in Egypt, which upheld the status of Aten; and because of this, because of the undying sacrifice and loyalty, *Aten would be satisfied*, he thought.

△△△

The exiles, for all of their effort, were unable to fulfill a sense of belonging and a sense of security and peace even after many years praising Aten. They were the seeds searching to germinate in a barren terrain but their efforts to become rooted in the place were frustrating and futile. In Egypt, they were the hated ones now, nomads in the wilderness grazing sheep and herding cattle. They became the nomadic shepherds the Egyptians despised, the nomadic shepherds they themselves despised.

Their monotheism provoked a deep hatred towards them for their belief in one god but also for the desecration of the ancient gods and holy places and for the killing of the beloved Tutankhamen, the peacemaker. In the face of it all, they continued to praise Aten and hope was all they had after thirteen years exiled in the Sinai. It was a hope they held on to lest they fail to strive and wither away.

Once the exiles arrived at the oasis in the Sinai where they built their own well, they stayed put for fear that if they journeyed back to Egypt without their leader, they would become weak and die of thirst. Egyptian sentries guarded those wells that were extended north in central Sinai and along the Horus Road from Egypt to Palestine, but Akhenaten could command water when presenting his scepter of royalty since no sentry would have the courage to deny a Pharaoh or a former Pharaoh.

Yet the wells were no river and the great river was Akhenaten's desire. So great was his desire that he himself began to wonder how much longer they could hold out in the Sinai. The yearning for home caused him to acknowledge the error of his ways as Aye predicted. Because it was obvious to him now that Aten was a tribal god and no god of the universe, which both he and his son made great efforts to achieve—Akhenaten by way of unbending command, Tutankhamen through peaceful concession.

Akhenaten would never compromise the sole status of Aten, but he thought he would disguise his true intentions now to bide time until he could once again seize power. He began to sense the time was right to reclaim the throne. Of course, he needed to convince the military that the temples of their respective villages would reopen; and he needed also to regain the trust of the nobility. Akhenaten and Ipy decided to pay a visit to Egypt to see them, the nobles and the military after the death of Aye.

"Ipy, we must go to the royal palace and reclaim the throne," said Akhenaten.

ΔΔΔ

Over the ensuing month as Akhenaten and Ipy made bold plans to seize the empty throne, a man named Horemheb seized upon an opportunity himself and put into place his own plan. The plan, although ambitious involved the crown of the Eighteenth Dynasty, which he hoped to make his own; and when he married the sister of Queen Nefertiti to legitimize his efforts, the general of Aye's military became king.

More rumors began to spread, of course, among the commoners and nobles concerning Aye's mysterious death. Instead of the exiled Akhenaten, they now blamed Horemheb for Aye's death, as the new king seemed to covet the throne all along. Some thought Horemheb colluded with the Amen priests who were content with the reign of Tutankhamen after the restoral of Amen but believed King Aye would soon set them back. That perhaps he would return to the old ways of Akhenaten, and that in itself was motivation for murder.

There was also a percolating doubt about Horemheb's loyalty to Aye, because, although he was part of the Eighteenth Dynasty, he was not from Amarna and did not share Aye's belief in the Aten. Regardless of the rampant rumors flying between the mouths of the commoners and the nobles, he was now king. And with the backing of the Amen priests and military, well entrenched, unless of course, he were to meet his mysterious death by another hand as well.

ΔΔΔ

Akhenaten and Ipy would decide on a different course of action. They waited a while before returning to Egypt to propose a compromise to Horemheb regarding the return of the Sinai exiles. They delayed their trip first to gather information about the political climate and behavior of the king from messengers or new exiles, and they were disappointed with the bad news. Horemheb outlawed monotheism and began to persecute Aten worshipers in Egypt; causing many to flee to the sanctuary of Nubia or Sinai to avoid his wrath.

Horemheb's actions were revenge for the killing of King Tutankhamen the peacemaker who returned reciprocity and balance to the land and the temples and gods to the people. Just as the stubborn Akhenaten learned the subtle art of compromise rather than force, the unreasonable Horemheb sought revenge and his revenge was nonnegotiable.

Horemheb like the majority of Egyptians was scornful towards Akhenaten because through his new monotheism, there was a general upheaval in Egypt of thousands of years of religious protocol. Aye's killing of the Sinai Atenists was never enough revenge for

Horemheb, who denied them their religion and tormented them as a matter of course in Egypt, and harassed them into harsh labor at the quarries.

Horemheb, angered at the mere thought of Akhenaten returning from Sinai to seek the throne, imposed a death penalty for anyone who spoke his name or the name of Aten. Sure enough, when a careless woman spoke the name of Akhenaten in a crowded market within earshot of some Amen priests, her punishment was death. He destroyed also the city of Amarna and its Aten temple and etched away from the monuments and holy places, all the names of Akhenaten and the Amarna legacy.

There was no rest for the weary at the quarries, for after the cutting of rock, they transported tons of it to the various building sites and many died from the work that was backbreaking and unending. Although the people hoped for some reprieve even to the point of developing a messianic nature—the idea of a redeemer come *again*—to liberate them from their state of dismal suffering—none, at least not Akhenaten, was forthcoming to save them during Horemheb's harsh rule.

Because he was Aye's general, Akhenaten misjudged Horemheb; hoping he would welcome the exiles back to Egypt. With the outlawing of Aten worship and the new policy of polytheism enacted by the new king, a return to Egypt meant certain persecution so their stubborn sacrifice in the Sinai continued.

"This king is unreasonable," said Ipy.

"The climate of Egypt under his rule is not suitable for our return," said Akhenaten.

"We must do something. The people are persecuted days upon days and unable to worship the Aten," said Ipy.

"He has chosen the side of the old ways but perhaps he will meet his demise, has Senen access to the palace?"

"No longer," said Ipy, "the entire Amarna court was replaced. It was the beautiful Senen I suppose who killed the royal taster instead of killing the king?" Ipy asked.

"It made available a useful pretext, in order to get even with the priests who placed fear into my mother's heart and threatened my death as I was in her womb," said Akhenaten.

"I had a notion all along my king, the evidence all pointed to Senen," said Ipy.

"It was my revenge; I have been fighting the Amen priests all along even from here in exile until my son betrayed me and conceded to them their power and the return of their god Amen. We can no longer fight from exile Ipy, but I will return us to the throne in due time," said Akhenaten.

The timing of the return to the throne was uncertain now, as Akhenaten and Ipy would remain exiled in the Sinai while Horemheb ruled for several years more.

ΔΔΔ

Then one day, good news arrived from a messenger. Horemheb the ruthless king was dead after thirteen years of rule and left no heirs to the throne. Akhenaten and Ipy would need to act fast as the messenger informed them that a man named Ramses, the general of Horemheb's army was planning to initiate the Nineteenth Dynasty—ending the Eighteenth.

"Where did you here of this?" Akhenaten asked of the messenger.

"From the humble peasantry my king— news filtered down from the nobles to the commoners, and then to the peasants very fast after the death of Horemheb," he said.

"Can it be true my king?" asked Ipy.

"It cannot be so Ipy for I am the son of Amenhotep, of the Eighteenth Dynasty. The Eighteenth Dynasty lives on through me and I shall claim the throne with my royal scepter," said Akhenaten.

"Yes my king even the sentries provide us water from the wells in view of the Pharaoh's scepter of royalty," said Ipy, "But who is this Ramses?"

"He is an old man like, if I may say so, the royal scribe," said the messenger.

The messenger was careful not to label the king an old man, even though he was old after twenty-six years exiled in the Sinai.

"Yes I know of him Ipy. Ramses, a life long member of the military even as I ruled. With certainty, he will recognize me as the living Pharaoh of the Eighteenth Dynasty."

Now without hesitation Akhenaten and Ipy prepared food and water for the journey to Egypt. They held out hope that Ramses had come up against opposition, which was always the case during a change in dynasties for this would delay his ascension with challenges from heirs and those pretending to be heirs. However, when a living Pharaoh challenges the legitimacy of a new dynasty, it becomes quite a significant matter. Akhenaten felt it was his birthright and his duty to do so, to challenge Ramses with his scepter of royalty and to prove his case as living heir.

Ipy was a strong witness as Akhenaten's royal scribe and member of the king's court and advisor to the king and he himself accompanied the king during their initiation into the temple for training.

"My king, we have come a long way since the day of our initiation," said Ipy as they began their journey to Egypt.

"We were neophytes Ipy, searching for knowledge in the temple," said Akhenaten.

"It was your vocation to give to the people one god, my king," said Ipy.

"Your skepticism was quite healthy," said Akhenaten, "thousands of years of religious protocol and the gods beloved by the people was much to overcome."

"When you take the throne my king, Aten will reign over Egypt and over the whole earth as the sole god," said Ipy.

"Yes my scribe, our little tribe of Atenists will grow and grow even beyond the borders of Egypt. We will spread the word of Aten to the four corners of the earth that he reigns over," said Akhenaten.

Ipy knew this familiar attitude of the king since childhood. He had his imperfections but to Ipy those were also strengths as his stubbornness enabled him to persevere and his hate toward his enemies equaled his capacity to love. Ipy witnessed many times as the king transformed his anger or resentment of the priests into a beautiful hymn to Aten. Yet, he also knew the former king tended to go far beyond the practical to praise and please the Aten as little else mattered to the king but the satisfaction of the god.

As young neophytes once upon a time, Akhenaten claimed it would be his vocation to rid Egypt of the ancient gods beloved by the people. There was no compromise in him as a prince and none as a king—he lacked balance, consideration, fairness and peace toward his neighbors when it came to Aten. Tutankhamen his own son the peacemaker tried in desperation to impose these qualities and died for doing so. Ipy in secret, believed Akhenaten was complicit in the murder of his own son, because he had the authority to stop it with a simple verbal command and did nothing.

Now when they command the throne once again and impose the will of Aten upon the land of Egypt, their tribe would increase tenfold and that thought lingered with Ipy for some time before he spoke.

"Yes, my king. We will grow our tribe and spread the word of Aten into Nubia, Libya, Palestine, Hatte, Assyria and Babylonia and to the sea people and to the shepherds," said Ipy.

ΔΔΔ

After three days journey, Akhenaten and Ipy reached the city of Thebes in Egypt and went right away to present their case against Ramses to the elders. At the meeting of elders, at a table where the elders sat between the two, the case of the true heir to the throne got underway. Akhenaten, now 64 years old, carried his scepter of royalty and presented it during the trial.

"I am the son of Amenhotep III and rightful heir to the throne of the Eighteenth Dynasty," said Akhenaten.

The scepter of royalty Akhenaten presented to the elders was the unmistakable staff of a Pharaoh. The brass handle in the shape of a cobra distinguished it from the ordinary shepherd's staff and caused ordinary people to tremble at the sight of it. Ramses was indifferent, however and refused to recognize Akhenaten as the former king, although he must have known since they were near the same age. He labeled Akhenaten a fraudulent pretender claiming to be the son of Amenhotep III and son-in-law of Yuya. Of course, if he admitted knowing him, it would have given credence to Akhenaten's claim to the throne.

"He has not the attire of a king and not a shaven beard yet he claims to be of royalty," said Ramses.

Akhenaten, as always in possession of his scepter of royalty started,

"I know of Ramses the lifelong military man, but he claims not to know me the son of Amenhotep and king of the Eighteenth Dynasty," said Akhenaten.

"I will here nothing more of the Eighteenth Dynasty. I am the king of the Nineteenth Dynasty, and I shall remain on the throne," said Ramses.

After much deliberation of the evidence, the elders decided in Akhenaten's favor, for with his scepter of royalty and several witnesses, including Ipy, he proved to be the son of Amenhotep III, and living heir of the Eighteenth Dynasty. Yet, Ramses refused to comply with the ruling of the elders; and with the firm backing of the military, which he himself commanded under Horemheb, he took over the throne and palace with force and became the first king of the Nineteenth Dynasty.

△△△

Almost two years had passed after the decision of the elders. Although many feared a rebellion led by Akhenaten, none was forthcoming for a rebellion would mean certain defeat at the hands of the powerful military. Since even a threat of rebellion could stir up dissent among the nobility who were also unhappy about his forceful taking of the throne, bloodshed would mean a political loss for Ramses also. Both leaders were open to compromise and Akhenaten proposed one after a veiled threat.

"The elders ruled in my favor and I am beloved by the Nubian Queen in the south and the nomadic shepherds of the east and you, Ramses lay in between," said Akhenaten.

"I'm afraid we have already secured diplomatic relations with the queen, a Nubian invasion is impossible. And the whole of Egypt would never stand for another invasion of shepherds after the Hyksos," said Ramses.

"There is no suggestion of that," said Akhenaten, changing his course, "we shall sojourn out of Egypt to the Sinai with all my people in Amarna, the quarries and those of Zarw, living near the city of Pi-Ramses, which they built for you. The Sinai is a land that is unused except for a few shepherds grazing their herds; we shall settle and worship in peace without rebellion or interference to the palace."

"Where do you propose to grow crops in such a desolate land?" asked Ramses.

Akhenaten himself wondered if the oasis near the foothills of Mount Sinai could sustain them, yet he had no choice but to go east to Sinai as Nubia, one of the traditional places of refuge, was no longer an option.

"From the quarries and from Amarna, we will go to Pi-Ramses near the northern border where the great River of Kush flows into the Mediterranean to meet the others wishing to sojourn with us," said Akhenaten.

After pacing the floor while considering the proposal, Ramses realized Akhenaten's move to Sinai would rid him of his challenger to the throne and all of the annoying heretics at last.

"Your request is now granted. Those from Amarna and the quarries and Pi-Ramses may join with you in the Sinai but you must never return and meddle in the affairs of the monarchy," said Ramses.

After Akhenaten convinced Ramses to allow the quarry workers and citizens of Amarna and Pi-Ramses safe passage to Sinai, he and Ipy staged the outcast quarry workers on the bank of the Nile near Thebes, and began their journey north to join with those from Amarna and Pi-Ramses.

△△△

Ramses was relieved to rid himself of the heretics and their god Aten after all the damage they had done in Egypt, as they would be harmless in Sinai, which was far away from Thebes. However, after three days on their journey, King Ramses had a change of mind after conferring with his general.

"They could join with foreign enemies at the north border and rebel against the king," said the general.

"Conspire with the enemy to overthrow the palace?" asked Ramses.

"Yes my king, and there are hundreds more that will join them in Sinai," said the general.

"Akhenaten himself hinted at a possible link up with Nubia and shepherds from the east," said Ramses.

"Then my hunch is correct my king, the hated shepherds, strangers to us, will also join them," said the general.

"They'll not live another day to rebel against the king. We will pursue them and slaughter them at the sun's rising," said Ramses.

Ramses ordered the general to prepare a regiment of charioteers and the next morning would go in pursuit of the Atenists advancing toward Pi-Ramses. When a soldier still loyal to Akhenaten heard of the murderous plans, he went ahead that night to inform him, Akhenaten, before the scheduled pursuit by the military the next morning.

"They will come at sunrise," said the soldier.

"We cannot continue to Pi-Ramses. We must cross the narrow inlet of the sea, toward Sinai," said Akhenaten, "perhaps it will hinder the pursuit of the chariots."

"We'll have children and elders with us on this journey, they could drown crossing the sea without a boat," said Ipy.

"I know the narrow inlet well. The area is marshy and thick with mud and three feet of water at low tide," said the soldier.

"Are you certain?" asked Ipy as he looked toward the moon to see that it was one quarter of its full size.

"It is true," said another, "now that the tide is low, it's a marshy muddy shortcut to Sinai but it will rise again to eight feet with the waxing tide."

"We will go east to cross the sea," said Akhenaten, "Ipy go with the soldier on his chariot to Pi-Ramses and gather those willing to join us. Then return south till you reach the marshy crossing; and meet with us there by nightfall."

"From Pi-Ramses we could take the Road of Horus," said Ipy.

"The marshy crossing of the sea will hinder the chariots, but on the road, there's a chance they could apprehend you," said Akhenaten.

Because Pharaoh Ramses went back on his word to allow safe passage to the sojourners, thousands once hopeful to live and worship in peace now must flee for their lives toward the marshy inlet of the Red Sea to avoid capture. Ipy was on his way to Pi-Ramses one hundred miles north before returning back south to meet with Akhenaten and the others.

Akhenaten was convinced at the time that he could out maneuver Ramses because they started their journey from the quarries near Thebes on the east bank of the Nile and had a three-day head start. Although Ramses and his military would come fast on their chariots at sunrise, Akhenaten knew they were unaware of the change in direction and in all probability would continue north toward Pi-Ramses.

The next day, however, the new path taken became obvious to the pursuing Ramses as the sojourners left their imprinted tracks from the south and tracks from the north, which met in the middle and turned east toward the Red Sea. Then Ramses went east himself toward the sea in rapid pursuit of the heretics lest they live and return to topple the throne.

△△△

With each laborious step, the sojourners—some carrying old men, women and children on their backs, started across the marshy inlet of the sea at low tide through a thick sinking mud.

As the tide increased, the water reached the shoulders of the remaining few who heard the horses and chariots approaching like thunder before they could see them, then behind them, chariot after chariot splashed into the sea.

At first with solid footing near the shore, they made steady progress, the chariots, but midway across the hooves of the horses and encumbered wheels of the chariots became stuck in the mud due to the weight. The soldiers attempted to swim but their heavy battle armor weighed them down. Their efforts to stay afloat were futile as they splashed about and groped at the thin air in desperation. Ramses and his soldiers drowned in the unforgiving marshy trap and waxing tide of the sea.

From the safety of the seashore, now that Akhenaten and his followers witnessed the drowning of Ramses and all of his men and horses, he knew he could never return to the oasis at the foot of the Mount Sinai. The place would never sustain them as they numbered now in the thousands and the Egyptians would seek revenge for the death of Ramses.

"Ipy we must distance ourselves from our Egyptian enemies and go east out of Sinai to a fertile land to settle and grow crops," said Akhenaten.

"Yes my king, I will send messengers to the mount to inform the rest to join us on our journey," said Ipy.

In preparation for their continued sojourn toward a fertile more promising land that could sustain their numbers at a safe distance from those set on revenge, they filled all of their pottery and all of their vessels labeled with Egyptian hieroglyphs with water from a well in route to the Road of Horus.

After reaching the well with no sentries guarding it, Akhenaten, Ipy and a few of the shepherds filled their vessels with water. But as a shepherd turned the pulley to retrieve a fourth vessel of water, a sentry patrolling on his chariot arrived.

"We warned you shepherds to stay away from the wells," said the sentry.

"This is no shepherd. This is a Pharaoh," said Ipy.

When Akhenaten displayed his scepter of royalty, the sentry who was skeptical of the man Ipy claimed to be a Pharaoh in the company of shepherds, bowed at the sight of it. Although it was his duty to question Akhenaten, he refrained from doing so as it was never wise for a sentry to confront a Pharaoh.

Later, a royal messenger delivered the news to Seti about the death of his father Ramses and about a Pharaoh and his shepherds tapping water from the wells. Now Seti would be king, but before his coronation and even before he mourned the death of Ramses, he went to Sinai to confront this Pharaoh and his shepherds.

From Thebes, he and his soldiers followed the Red Sea north until they spotted several chariots with horses and soldiers bobbing in the mucky waters along the shore. The faces of the drowned soldiers, swollen and nibbled away by fish looked similar to one another until there was discovered the face of an elder man that could be none other than Ramses who was in his sixties.

"They murdered my father the king," said Seti, "gather the body and return it to Thebes."

I will avenge the death of Ramses, Seti thought as he watched the soldiers gather up his dead father, and off he went in pursuit of the sojourners.

Seti was weary of the bothersome shepherds stealing water from the wells and now they went so far as to demand it from the sentries, with a so-called Pharaoh in their company possessing a scepter of royalty. This situation, in combination with the death of his father Ramses, compelled Seti to pursue them and to finish them at last.

Seti went in pursuit from a distance, as a determined Akhenaten climbed the foothills of the mountain overlooking the land of Palestine, which bordered Sinai, to discern the best route to enter it with the least possible resistance. His scepter of royalty, a remnant from the glory days of Amarna, pierced the earth step after step up the mountain. As he climbed higher, he could see a great distance and it became obvious that the military could block them along the Road of Horus at the border of Palestine. Then he looked toward the east and discovered an alternative route near the River Jordan.

As he beheld the fertile land of Palestine, he was unaware of the carnage below him at the foot of the mountain. His followers were under attack by Seti's military. The soldiers wielded arrows, swords and battle-axes and maimed or killed hundreds. Yet as the blood flowed, Seti climbed the mountain in pursuit of the exiled Pharaoh.

He sought to protect his throne because Akhenaten challenged his father and feared he would do the same to him. There was also the heresy, turmoil and upheaval, the man in his sights wrought upon Egypt. There was also the matter of avenging the death of Ramses and most important, retrieving the scepter of royalty, for the old monotheist ascending the mountain was no longer a king but a shepherd leading a now scattered flock below him.

Seti readied his battle-ax as he approached and went on the attack without hesitation while Akhenaten stood viewing the land of Palestine. A startled Akhenaten turned just as Seti sent the ax down upon him with much force, and the heretic king managed to parry the blow with his scepter of royalty. Another blow unleashed by Seti was from the side, striking the king in the rib cage and causing him to drop his scepter and fall to the ground. Akhenaten scratched and clawed in an effort to retrieve the scepter. But as he reached out in desperation Seti stood on it and unleashed a fatal blow on the king's skull—killing him on the slope of the mountain.

After the death of Akhenaten, his followers remained many years in the Sinai wilderness. Later, they sojourned to Palestine to settle and carried with them a hieroglyphic scroll in praise of their lord in heaven along with pottery and water vessels decorated with the hieroglyphic writings of their Egyptian past.

www.ingramcontent.com/pod-product-compliance
Lightning Source LLC
Chambersburg PA
CBHW02065526026
47157CB00008B/3036